Stephanie Klein is a cheerleader for surrealism's role in confounding the logic of capitalism. Yet *Planetoid Sassafras* rather is the logic of capitalism: life reduced to the mindless, compulsive stroking of sensory receptors, oblivious to all else, even if it means *the end of life*. And it goes one better than that: there is none of capitalism's suffocating sameness to be found here. *Planetoid Sassafras* is marvelous, hilarious, frightening and—its only real affinity with capitalism— hypnotic. It is an "Ero-Death cosmology", perhaps best read while seated in a moldy-rice-stuffed chair, the book held at eye-level by a dead, spotted hand.

- Patrik Sampler, author of *The Ocean Container*

Listen up meatbrains and unzipped larval spongeforms. This book of schizocompressed visioning is as beautiful as luminous neon fleshtrees, scantily clad corneas, dark fecal explosions, and giggling fishes merrily surfing gelatinous waves under ejaculating green skies. Better than a local performance of "Traditional Intestinal Theatre"!

- Ron Sakolsky, author of
Scratching the Tiger's Belly & Seizing the Airways

If H.P. Lovecraft were to be kidnapped by a reptilian army, fed psilocybin from a trashcan, butt-fucked by the animated corpse of Georges Bataille, and impregnated with his own gut flora, he might finally give birth to a shuddering ball of hot space rock called *Planetoid Sassafras*. Resistance to Stephanie Klein is futile. Sure, she has some unhygienic ideas, and she's not entirely trustworthy. But once she's had her way with you, you'll be glad you surrendered.

- Merl Fluin, author of *The Golden Cut*

Planetoid Sassafras

ISBN: 978-1-940233-62-8

Cover, interior art © 2019 Casi Cline

Design © 2019 Rick Febré

Montag Press Team:

Project Editor – Charlie Franco

Managing Director – Charlie Franco

A Montag Press Book

www.montagpress.com

Montag Press

777 Morton St. Unit B

San Francisco CA 94129

Montag Press, the burning book with the hatchet cover, the skewed word mark and the portrayal of the long-suffering fireman mascot are trademarks of Montag Press.

Printed & Digitally Originated in the United States of America

10 9 8 7 6 5 4 3 2 1

This book is a work of fiction. Names, characters, places, and incidents are either products of the author's vivid and sometimes disturbing imagination or are used fictitiously without any regards with possible parallel realities. Any resemblance to actual persons, living or dead, events, or locales is entirely coincidental.

Many thanks to Casi and Jason,
for their constant support, insight, and inspiration.

for the amorous & amorphous leopard slug

STEPHANIE KLEIN

Planetoid Sassafras

MONTAG

Introduction

When in 1818 the utopian philosopher Charles Fourier completed his unpublishable treatise on the pleasures of the future, The New Amorous World, it is not impossible that he had already visited Planetoid Sassafras. While we can prove nothing, all of the internal evidence seems to indicate that he in fact did so: the strange, passional world, the variety of awe-inspiring flora and fauna, the growth of frightening new capabilities, organs, senses, erogenous social structures, gastronomies, varieties of orgy—in short the unbridled sexual liberation, not only of humanity, or what was once humanity, but nature itself, the planets, the stars and moons... Could it be that he may only have mistaken the displacement in location for a displacement in time? That what he foresaw so hopefully for the earth was really the strange signal of an alien body, far away in the cosmos? Or are we the ones who are mistaken? Internal conviction will confirm it readily enough. Simply look at the stars, dear reader, and then at your own sex—do you perceive the milky stream of planetary ectoplasm connecting the two?

Such evidence as well as the natural lusty proclivities of every passional subject will confirm that this is not to be a taken as a fictional story, but a factual account. The author can in no way be accused of the usual flights of fancy present in science fiction or pulp fantasy, for here we find nothing but a sober journalist coolly reporting on the facts found—a Humboldt or a Darwin, a biologist and natural historian rather than a mere scandalous raconteur. And yet, while coolly observing the firm, purposeful grip of Zjracnim and the ASTRAL GEISHA, the quivering of member and aperture in philosophical resonance—can you blame even the most stoic observant for falling prey to the seductions of such a world? A lapse of a second or a thousand years, it makes no difference: a journey to Planetoid Sassafras will forever change the way you lust.

Astronomically speaking, it is unclear from its description whether Sassafrass is a "planet" proper, or some asteroid or other cosmic body. The different sections of the book range from the initial tour of the planetoid to odd poetic rhapsodies about sacs and fungi, afternoons spent among miniatures, pits and bellies, evenings at the intestinal theatre... all pointing to different potential interpretations. As such there have been a few theories as to its possible location. Many are based on the vivid but ambiguous sexual-planetary relations described in the book itself. Others, such as that of the distinguished professor of microerotics Mortiz Fuchs, claim that Sassafras displays all the characteristics of certain tropical extremophilia located at the bottom of ocean vents. Still others have searched for it in terrariums filled with slugs and insects, in the physiological systems of nudibranchs, or even in the living works of certain odd surrealist collagists and painters. I have my own theory that Sassafrass is encoded in our DNA, creating a correspondence between individual hominids and the wider occult world of attraction. But one thing is certain: whoever the author is, whatever their number, however they ooze, the future sciences of pain and pleasure surely owe them a great debt.

A final note on the word "erotic". This word would be the one typically applied to the kind of steamy pulp fare this book is no doubt being marketed as—and yet despite the lurid hopes of the perverse booksellers, this word is in no way sufficient to the sensations to be found herein. Instead, we must turn to the work itself to find a suitable term, a master-word to govern erotic impulse of this new world: fuckcontagion. An alchemical marriage of disease and desire into a single ungovernable impulse. Ah reader, enjoy your stay: but don't get too near, for we are fuckcontagious too…

    -J. Abdelhadi, surrealist and editor at *Peculiar Mormyrid*

Table of Contents

Planetoid Sassafras

Our st*ory takes place on a rather normal Unday,*
in pleasantly bright Month of Pan.
The year is 3731 A.M.
*   (Your portable knowledgepack suddenly chimes in:*
*   "Hi Reader! This is your helpful informational interlude! I scanned*
your adorable little meatbrain just now and saw you were missing some
helpful facts. The marker A.M., or After Marx, is the most widely ac-
cepted standard in this particular galactic sector. The Earthen A.D., B.C.,
and C.E. are currently unfashionable on Planetoid Sassafras and are only
used by one illegally imported Galapagos tortoise, who stubbornly refuses
to part with Anno Domini. An incredibly mean and reactionary old fellow,
that one! The bastard just won't die!"
*   You (Dear Reader) think that this portable knowledgepack is extreme-*
ly annoying, and decide to go at the story alone. You switch off its power
source and throw the pesky new tech into the garbage. Oh cocky reader, are
you really sure about this? Trying to read a story without help from even
one cyber outmind?! Even a cheap, off-brand one would be better than div-
ing in these words cerebrally naked! —Ah, but it's too late. You aren't even
reading me anymore; you've walked off in a huff. So be it.)

Zjracnim woke up on the morning of the second sun. Ze
was feeling very frisky. Zir naked anatomy was feeling a bit
chilled, especially the drooping intestines, so ze opened up zir
dresser drawer and pulled out a tight green and red skin-suit.
It was a scale-based reptilian piece, a fungal growth freshly cut
from a juvenile fleshtree on Moon 12. Little circles covered
the skin, dark red around the edges and almost white in the
centers. The presentation looked very pretty and chic to zim,

almost like one of those fashionable new skin diseases worn by young Sassafrasians. Rashes and hives were very "in" this year on Sassafras, part of a long-standing trend towards humanoid disease appropriation. Oddly enough, the humanoids themselves did not yet appreciate the unique aesthetic beauties of their bodily degradations. What a magnificent flesh diversity there was to be found on Earth, what amazing asymmetry! Here on Sassafras, corruption of flesh was all too rare, our orderly bodies completely lacking in surprise, most likely due to an unfortunate shortage of microbes in this sector.

Zjracnim finished dressing and walked out the door of zir sentient cocoonroom, accidentally hitting zir long furry ears on the moaning ceiling above as ze ducked through a low hanging door. The walls of zir room oozed out droplets of sticky marshmallow cum at Zjracnim's soft touch. Oh well, Ze would scrub it all up later…Constant seminal fluid cleanups were just the unavoidable fact of life at that flat, zir sentient cocoonroom existing as it did in an unending state of almost-orgasm. Ze'd heard that the original architect had had much trouble in getting these rooms to multiply at first, and under pressure from the impatient property manager had been forced to inject a powerful dose of the (then recently discovered) "pervert gene" into the building's flesh in order to coax its "lazy" rooms into spawning. The landlord had ended up having to lower his rates after all the semen leaking complaints however, and a good riddance to the old penny-pinching bastard.

The Commune had taken over the block centuries ago, though. There was no longer an economic system of Capootoejizm on planetiod Sassafrass. After the revolution, The Commune had banished the leftover upper classes, him included, into the dark underworld burrows of the Monstrous Mycelium, and zeir bodies were torn limb from limb by collections of long-suffering filaments and alienated spores. Later, a reanimated and newly class-conscious Zosimos had transmuted zeir limbs into a tasty peanut butter paste in order to feed the starving hordes of earthworm proletariat. As for zose unlucky rich who had managed to escape to their seaside villas in the revolutionary confusion, zey were later discovered and thrown to the mercies of the grim Madreporic Army Faction, the MAF, and were never seen or heard from again. I shudder to think!

Anyhow, for a few years now ze had lived in this slow-growing fleshcastle flat. Ze felt it to be a low-key, quiet sort of place, populated mainly by aging Sassafrasians. It had a lovely view, too. Zir room overlooked that fabulous ocean of pink pus, the old Pustular Pacifika. This ocean was a popular tourist destination, especially among the luminous aggregations of Orgone families in the summertime. It was almost off-season now though, and the crowd on the beach was small. Ze quickly made zir way down the rocky stairway toward the beach, jumping eagerly over the last few steps. Ze tripped on impact and fell into the sand with a giggle. Ze then picked zirself up off the ground, brushing off the sticky little greenish grains of sand trying to burrow themselves into zir skin.

"Not today, friends," ze said with a smile. Ze wasn't ready for a sand-birthing today; ze was in the mood for a completely different sort of fornication. Ze desperately needed invasion by a new fetishform, but ze wasn't sure what that was yet. Ze kept walking, zir square, goat-like pupils eagerly searching the marvelous, pastel green horizon. Ze was beach-combing for a fresh fuckcontagion; ze was looking for a defilement from an overflowing new energy source. Zir pieced and split penis was half-erect, and zir gina-grafts were pulsating. The randomly spaced vulvas on zir back were also leaking so profusely that a casual onlooker might even think ze'd broken out in a sweat...

Coming to the edge of the purple waters, ze looked up, and the green sky ejaculated. Lusty ol' Moon 13 had once again crossed paths with the coquettish Moon 5, and they had greedily copulated. In 1/19 of a second the cosmic sex-fertilization-birth process had produced Moon 109898329. A promiscuous one, that Moon 13! Quite the Don Juan! As they would've said in olden times. A deafening and irritatingly familiar moonbaby cry echoed out across the planet Sassafras, causing sassy old men and women everywhere to grumble to themselves and turn up the volume on their ancient Televizor sets.

The newly born moony bastard would likely be sent away to float above some savage Sector 57 frontier town. Many in the commune felt the Sassafras skyline to be rather overly moon-full these days, though Moon-exiling was still a major point of contention at the recent assemblies...

Finally the moon baby's cries stopped, and Zjracnim's headache began to subside. Ze peeled off zir single-use viscous noise canceling ear covering and threw it down on the beach. The sand grains devoured the plastic object within seconds, and defecated a larval swarm of rainbow-striped gastropods. Alchemical matter transmutations were just a fact of life here on delightful Sassafras, and "littering" was encouraged.

Zjracnim strolled on down the beach, waving at zir gelatinous blobite friend Billzie and a few of the other fish-egg-expectorating regulars along the way. It sure was hard being one of the Catfish-descended Sassafrasians, ze mused. So much time spent vomiting those translucent eggs, and never even really knowing if some horny nudibranchen will come along to fertilize them! Zeir schoolbooks explained that the Sassafrasian Catfish creatures had mutated from a batch of Earth specimens long ago, caught somewhere in that rich planetary habitat called "Deep South" by some extrater-restrial angler. Or was it from a batch found in "Okratic Flor-didia"? Though maybe that was just a sub-region under the taxonomic umbrella of "Deep South"? Whatever, Zjracnim wasn't much for interplanetary ecology, and especially not dull "Earth" stuff. Ze kept zir two slimy feet on the ground, and zir thoughts on zir native Sassafras. Those were subjects better left to the protoplasmic bloodkites, those lucky bastards born with a parasitic master's degrees ameboidically lodged on the underside of their placentas.

The bright orange fish eggs continued to sweep across large expanses of that section of beach, bouncing about in the wind like an army of wayward spit bubbles. They looked to Zjracnim rather sad and pitiful, and yet spongily beautiful too.

Ze walked past a small purple tide pool, its spiraling drift-wood and dead jellies bobbing in the tide. The floating bits and bobs suddenly snapped themselves together, forming a large swimming eye. It winked at zir seductively. Was this the chance encounter ze had been looking for? Ze lilliputianed zir perception box and dropped down inside Surrconscious. Ze then fast-travelled via the quantum metro, almost running off the rails in a mad dash to the center. Reaching the unseen side, ze consulted the wise intuit-tubes hanging from the Lighthouse Keeper's groin, suctioning out a load of stringy blue prophecy with zir mouth. But when ze read the squirming blue fortune cookies they all said "NO." Ze sidestepped out of Halfworld, zir taut bodythought expectorating into the waiting arms of OutWorld. Disappointment was the word.

Ze politely tipped zir furry ears to the expectant tide pool and walked on. Ze went north. Ze followed close to the line of the thick pustule ocean now, and watched as the gelatinous waves fell and rose in slow motion—a kind of fetid aquatic molasses. Swimming in it was a rather tricky business, best left to professionals and the foolhardy. As a child, ze had often gotten the ocean stuck up zir nose while diving for red pearls, and zir left nostril would drip with pink pus for weeks. It was hard to stomach its overpowering smell, too.

After a half hour had passed, Zjracnim began to feel more buoyant. After all, the weather really was quite magnificent today, and what a pleasant breeze there was! Ze decided to compose a few Sassafrasian poems in zir head as ze walked. It was a goofy little pastime that ze sometimes enjoyed, but was very embarrassed by to share publicly. As a result ze anonymously posted some fragments of them on the etherweb sometimes, although zir rebirthing mother and pet caterpillar had no idea of zir literary pretensions. They were both rather judgmental when it came to the proper usage of Sassafrasian poeyforms; and recent trends towards a grammatical tumor harvest and a fleshy word copulation were still unheard of in their more elevated circles.

In any case, Zjracnim's new beach poem went like this:

Oh, to ejaculate a DoorWand!
Go eat that red black corridor, if you please
And don't stop for a passing amoeba
In other words
The Purple Jelly is best eaten on cloudbread
With a dead hand covered in spots
—and no Biscuit?

Ze wasn't sure if it was any good. Ze was never sure. It got filed away in the brain bank anyway, listed under the subheading "DoorWand Erotica."

Suddenly zir's skinscale colony began to vibrate and ripple across zir chest. Ze heard long and satisfied sighs, coming from somewhere in the vicinity of zir crotch. And some outbreaks of impish laughter, too. Possibly zir suit had been acting like this for a while and ze hadn't even noticed it, distracted as ze was by the intricacies of Sassafrasian poetics. The skin's shaking movement quickened the farther north ze walked. Zir suit seemed to have become magnetized, reacting to an unseen flesh-force. But who?

Ze looked around nervously. At the curve of the shoreline ze noticed that a large mound had appeared. It was barely discernable at this distance, but seemed vaguely meat-based and aquatic to Zjracnim's straining eye. A beached leviathan perhaps? Some diabolic inhabitant from the as-yet-unexplored Great Pustacular Trench? The air surrounding the creature looked a shade darker, too. The bright-pastels and neons of the world seemed to drain.

It lookedfelt to zim like a twitching aggregation of little void dots:

A Hyper-Occulted Black Mass & a Bottomless Obsidian Swarm

Ze felt that the dark cloud's three physical processes could be identified as:

A) a dribbling

B) a wriggling

C) a defiling

And there were three things that the black cloud could be:

A) Empyrean conjuration from moist astroidal slit

B) The Sidereal Pudenda

C) An Elder God's poorly thought out "come-hither"

(But also, truthfully speaking, possibly none of these things)

Was it all a glitch in zir vision? A glitch in Zireality itself? Ze asked zir sentient metatarsals to fleshform thirteen dwarf hooves for added acceleration, and then rushed towards the seductive mass at full gallop, zir eyes filling with lust. Zir mad

rush caused a few of these fragile new dwarf hooves to shatter along the way, leaving behind a dangerous trail of broken
fleshglass on the beach – but that was normal.

*"My god, but what if someone came along and stepped on that!" you,
Dear Read, think, wringing your weak and fleshy humanoid hands. And
you prepare to heroically jump inside this cruel narrative with dustpan and
broom. "Gotta clean it up before someone gets hurt!" you say to yourself
full of privileged confidence.*

But, alas, it's already too late, the worst has already happened. A family of unsuspecting Nudibranchs have already
rolled over the sharp debris. The translucent little shards cut
deep inside their soft mollusk bodies, clinging tightly to their
undersides and piercing their delicate organs with each oozing
movement. The sunlit beach is filled with cries of gastropod
agony.

"What a splendid, beautiful pain!" squealed the old sluggy
patriarch.

*Confused, I can hear you, Dear Reader, asking Papa Slug if they
need any help.*

Try, but he will wave you away dismissively, saying:

"Actually, we're on our way to audition for a Vaporwave
remake of Salò, so this was the best possible outcome for us,
really! Mr. Pasolini will certainly appreciate our dedication to
the role."

*Disheartened, you shrug your shoulders and jump back out of the story.
You resolve (with mild irritation) to never "Play Hero" in a surrealist
narrative ever again...to which we all whole-heartedly agree. Hurrah!*

As for our main character whom you've been so quick to forget about —

The ol' excitable Zjracnim had almost reached the dark leviathan. Zir penis was massively erect and flapping in the wind
like a sack of sprouting potatoes or a sock filled with moldy rice.
A long stream of zir vaginal juices trailed behind. What a gem

our Zjracnim is! A real fine fellow!

Listen, here's a bit of added Zjracnim backstory for y'all, since I know earthlings prefer stories with rich character histories.

Our sweet-natured Zjracnim was born of an illegally imported orangutan mother. After her mandatory cyborgization, she self-impregnated with the then-popular mathematical formula of [male + female ÷ aardvark × syrup], a formula which has since been superseded in popularity by many more complex algebraic formulas of conception. Yes, our Zjracnim may not be the most refined structure available anymore, but that doesn't mean we should judge! It certainly explains more than a few of our character's personality quirks, in any case.

Oh my, take a look over there:

Ze had arrived. Ze stood exactly three feet from the majestically rotting, putrid corpse.

subsumed by it. This Sacramental leftover, this UNFATHOMABLE AQUATIC ARCHFIEND! It's looking like the DaveyJones apotheosis

<quite irreversibly>

At this exact moment, the Commune's tourism committee was placing an invisible placard in the sand. The spectralized sign was visible only to drifting phantoms and astrally projecting voyeurs. The text on the sign read:

BEWARE BEWARE
OGOPOGO RISING
SECURE YOUR FOOD
REPODUCTIVE ORGANS
AND ALL OTHER VALUABLES
IN BLUE CASKET
DO NOT APPROACH

Zjracnim, being neither an astral projector nor a ghost,

didn't see the hastily mounted warning. Ze likely would never have heeded it, anyhow. Zir skin was dripping with so much carnal wax at this point that ze was on the verge of sex-born internal combustion. Yes, the BodyMeat was now so thoroughly heated and erotically brainsick that ze couldn't have stopped zimself if ze wanted too. Instincts were taking over.

flesh calls out to flesh
flesh answers in sweat pus precum
by Formation of Desire-Egg and by hatching
by the ardor of Consecrated Placentas
& the sweetness of the hemoglobin

Zjracnim's expanded groin sack almost burst with premature ejaculate. With some effort, Ze managed to hold it back. Ze steadied zimself and began to climb up the side of the decaying behemoth. Its skin felt rough and warty in some spots, and soft and pliant in others.

(In Earth terms, for those of you from there struggling to keep up, you could say it was like an ugly toad crossed with an effeminate jellyfish).

A very pleasing cross-sensation was breezing coyly through zir happy synapses. What great tactile success!

No, that rare performance of earthworm suctioning that you may have seen in that viral video on the pleasure district of Galaxy 9 last cycle doesn't even come close to approximating this. Your well-moisturized naked mole rat apology that burrowed itself into a holographic ocean cervix two Saturn-evenings ago doesn't match this particular fleshfeel either—it's not even close. You'll just have to experience it yourself...

Zjracnim's foot suddenly gave way and fell through the creature's putrefied belly skin, discharging an obscene squishy-sloshy sound and an overpowering stink of death. This messy setback merely brought Zjracnim to even higher heights of anticipation and arousal. Ze pulled zir sticky foot out of the pit, wiping away the beast's offal as best ze could. Zjracnim soon became worried about the unstoppable bloating on zir third cock-ball. Ze detached it for now, thrusting it deep inside the ear canal of the creature for safekeeping. Ze really didn't want to have a complete skin rupture today, and that little guy just didn't know how to hold back. Ze decided ze will come back for him later, once he's cooled off a bit. He was lodged pretty tight down in there, so Ze didn't think he'd be able to run off. Wait, ze wondered, was the monster's earlobe blushing? It was hard for zim to tell.

When ze reached the top of zir leviathan-love, ze inspected the creature's gargantuan mouth, feeling ready for a shy first kiss. Ze gazed on the thick, yellow lips, looking big and puckered like a fish. Did ze see a little movement in them just now? Or was it just the vibration of zir steps? On the mouth's right side, a slow deathdecay process had formed a half-melted grin. A cosmic smirk. Then ze saw the brave crabs side-walking into the gaping mouth hole. They did not return. Ze looked into Leviathan's decagonal eyes. They did not look like any eyes Ze had ever seen. They were crisscrossed in ever-moving geometric lines and colors. At the center point of the eye, there was a predominance of purple, but in the outer regions there was constant unfoldment, a lively dance across the color spectrum. A Rainbowing Banquet for zir, and zir alone.

ahohahoh
the treasured lover's eyes
this uncanniness ÷ cold sore ÷ desire ÷ spit
big carrion eyeballs zigzagging
ever-enveloping
in serpentine hexagrams
& dead unLanguages
yes indeed
looky what this cat dragged in

the attempt at seduction now obvious
This here is his
SIGIL MEMBRANE SHIFT
and that there is his
PENETRATION COMMAND
Oh, leviathan!
I submit!

With the preliminaries of this erotic liaison out of the way, the Leviathan asked zir what they should use for a safe word.

"Fishy-Petunia, perhaps?" suggested Leviathan. "Fungi-Intifada?"

Zjracnim groaned loudly, yelled, "Fuck man, I don't need a goddamn safe word! I'm fuckin' hardcore!"

Was this delirium the result of a (possibly fatal) outbreak of *masculine bravadoicus* inside the brain of our previously so likable hero? Unfortunately, recent infections have shown that even the Sassafrasians are not exempt from the despicable humanoid virus. Would zir naive extraterrestrial immune system be able to triumph over the abominable macho-plague?

After zir outburst, zir face looked calm and content, as if ze'd blown zir load. It looks like zir immune system has been victorious!

(Quick update. Zijracnim's Immune System has taken us both aside for a second, and is politely letting us know that she'd prefer to go by her new name "Immutiny," in reference to her anarchist ideals and general anti-authoritarian tendencies.)

Immutiny laid out a five second bout of amnesia on zir, and the weird outburst was emailed over to offices of braindeletion, where it was swiftly dealt with via an embarrasment-guillotine. We are receiving word that the now-empty *masculine bravadoicus* plague vessels were collected at the center of Cortex Town and are being burned together in a great bonfire. Reports suggest that Immutiny and her cellular pals danced merrily round the rising flames while singing of revolution, and the sweet-toothed neurons melted marshmallows galore.

"Why don't we use Kitten-Pastry as the safe word?" purred the foxy Zjracnim, and winked.

"What a relief," thought Leviathan. "Now that the trouble-some pathogen has been rejected, on to the main event!"

Zjracnim lay down on Leviathan, zir rear expectant-ly raised and shivering with anticipation. The ginas growing along zir back began to twitter and sing, performing for those watching like happy birds at an erotic sunrise. The beast's phal-lic sack was beginning to look engorged. With grasping ten-tacles, he reached down and unzipped his fleshy alembic, re-leasing the trapped penis from its long bondage. His prick was feeling rather thirsty now; and he decided to raise it up into the clouds for a few sips of rain. This was a big mistake. A pathetic sequence of events now unfolded: first, he tickled the wings of an asexual bird who wanted absolutely nothing to do with pricks, which then crashed into a Commune spaceship, and that ended by breaking apart into a gaseous hive of peaceable chemtrail spirts (who had never harmed a soul, conspiracies be damned).

A rather unwelcome encounter for all!

The leviathan felt incredibly embarrassed, even threaten-ing to swear off beach nudity for good, and Zjracnim tried zir best to comfort him. They had a little cry about it, and soon put the whole dreadful incident behind them. Hoping to get this sexual liaison back on track, Zjracnim assumed the posi-tion once more, zir body low and plump ass flying high. Levi-athan reached down inside his rotting chest and pulled out a pile of crimson arterial ropes and stool-swollen intestines. He tied Zjracnim up with the mushy cords, and covered zir face with a golden mask.

Well, now that you ask - It was a Sassafrasian forgery of the Mask of Agamemnon, if you really must know. Very fashionable in the BDZM circles around here.

Zjracnim barked like a dog, a parrot, and finally a snake. Ze rubbed zir nose in Leviathan's crotch, greedily licked it, and howled. Zir body began to leak out spongy white globs of Submission-Concept from zir pores, the fetishform made suddenly corporeal by such a successful dramaturgy. Leviathan pulled off the creamy mass and rubbed it across his face, passionately spreading it like viscous new makeup. His presence was soon changed, reforming underneath the sticky white paste. He rode the chrysalitic transference wave, switching gender lanes like a pro. The bystanders were shocked—as it all happened so suddenly. It was the becoming of ASTRAL GEISHA.

Matter Reconfiguration, you are the ultimate aphrodisiac!

Our newborn ASTRAL GEISHA gripped her penis in hand, guiding it to Zjracnim's anxiously waiting anal aperture. She thrusted in deep, penetrating through zir belly, zir throat, zir fragile skull. An explosion of blood, cum, and brain matter bounced out from Zjracnim's little head, the event barely registering on our disoriented minds as the prick accelerated. This diabolic phallus was now completely frozen inside an unstoppable *Down-Going* movement. It broke through planetary cores, galaxies, and multiverses. An infinite penis thrust, leaving behind galaxy-wide chaos and a wrecked space economy. And who would comfort all the depressed hordes of mourning StarWhale? They'd already clogged Planet Freud with all their problems.

When will the rest of us fuckups get a hit of that psychiatry, eh? That's what I'd like to know. I needed to disgorge! That dumb prick probably didn't even know that comet was your home when he destroyed it.

Probably.

Our adventurous Penis soon ruptured through the last re-maining retaining wall at the edge of spaceform, shooting out into that measureless Void of Time above the black cosmic ocean. Leviathan's body was so stretched out at this point that Penis was pulled loose from its bodybase. At this exact moment, Penis also decided to climax. Blood-tinted semen rushed out from the tip, our noble prick's orgasm farewell

.Penis continued on his downward tumble through weird-space. He wondered to himself how long he might have before his impact with the dreadful ocean below, that dark eldritch fluid filling up his vision, that strange aquatic obscenity driving him to the very brink of madness…

What horrors lie in its depths?

A loud crack was heard from within Penis. His body broke apart, dissolving like a luminous blood comet falling through the atmosphere.

Something to do with the abnormal air pressure down there? Perhaps.

A pinky mass of deconstructed prick continued its decent towards the black ocean. The ocean rushed up to meet it. To devour.

And now, Dear Reader, imagine this: your cybernetic view screen sud-denly goes blank.

Nothing but digital fuzz.

Nothing on the Com, either.

"Penis!" you yell.

"Penis, are you there?!? Answer me, Penis! Say something goddammit!"

It's no use kid, he's gone. Dead as a rock.

You've gotta move on now, kid.

And ya better get used to it too,

cuz life among genitals is cruel cruel cruel.

One disorienting spatial drop and a few roundabout mind-waves later…

…And we're back on Planetoid Sassafrass.

Zjracnim picked zirself up and gathered the stray bits of brainstuff scattered around. Ze popped them back in zir head hole, sealing the skull with a bit of spearmint gum and raw pseudohoney. Ze also reached down into zir throat and reassembled the prick-displaced organs. Good as new. Ze gave a deep, contented sigh.

Zir Leviathan lover was barely moving below zir, but there was a deep smile on her fishy lips. She seemed lost in a fog of pain and post-coital bliss, and her ASTRAL GEISHA sexform seemed to be ebbing, theatrical femininity slowly lost as her pale face melted under the bright Sassafrasian sun. Long trails of liquefying white ooze dripped down the monster's face, gradually revealing that dead yet lovable old sea god beneath.

Zjracnim loved the monster in all its many forms.

Loved the changeling genders, improvisations, moultings.

Embraced the Great Genital Transsubstantiation.

Our joyful Zjracnim cried—

"Cocooning is the great yes-saying! Cocooning is life!"

Yes, as you've seen here in this story, cocooning really is the next best thing. With each and every fuck we will pursue the philosopher's stone of the mucus membrane, creating our new lives within a Venereal Metallurgy. We will break these limited material bodies upon the wheels of cellular invocation, discovering each forgotten ecstasy & vice within.

Ze couldn't wait for the next transmutation.

"Embrace the intersphincteric mind and be set free."

Thus Spake Pudenda & Prick.

Metallurgy

Lilith called the community together and sang out the newsflash. A metal egg had been found in the desert; it was hot to the touch and ribbed like a vertebrate. It was spherical rather than ovoid. The men jumped on their domesticated caterpillars and jabbed their pitiful creatures with a specially designed riding needle to get them to full gallop. The women melted into shadows and became red vocal sighs in the wind. When they had all reached the clearing and saw the silver egg, they saw that it grew and shrank, breathing like an exhausted animal's abdomen after too much play. The men felt very aroused, and the women smiled secretively in the breeze circling above.

The egg said, "Whosoever can speak to me in a language undebased may have me."

A man with a frog's face pulled a moist and well-loved copy of Dante's works from his underwear. He read passage after passage from it—even including his absolute favorite verses, which he had underlined in dark blue ink and marked with a purple star—but was met with cold, steely, silence from the egg.

Next, the spectral women sang a little ditty about the movement of the stars and the menses of Jupiter's children, but were only received with a few skeptical "Hmms."

Then a little boy stepped forward, holding a pocketknife in one hand and an oyster shell in the other. Where he came from no one was quite sure. He began to skin himself. First hesitantly, and then with more courage, he sliced layer after layer of pink from his fragile young body. Reaching the penis, he paused momentarily, spat saliva inside the urethral opening, and began the Great Work. Blood pooled around him, drowning entire civilizations of desert grub and sentient cauliflower in tidal waves of warm, bodily juices. An IWW lumberjack's rusty bow saw, which had gone missing since the forgotten Portland wormhole strike of the early 1920s, space-shifted underneath the boy's crotch, its saw-teeth pointed up and the boy pressed down *hard* on it. Like a log, he rubbed his perineum back and forth on it. He screamed on it. The red, fluidic sweetness of his anatomy caused the metal egg to finally give birth to a majestic white horse with two X chromosomes. The horse called out to him in the coded language of extracellular fluids, a language only she and the boy could understand. *Corpus cavernosum. Genital tubercle. Erogenous zone.* A new ero-language, untainted by capitalism had been invented. Their bodies were not bodies and not spirit. They were neither but nowhere.

A flea lodged inside the tissue of a leprosy snout.

"…and inside the vertebrae of the horse, that old abused word, 'Liberty,' finally shed its skin and became a new and freer vocalization, transformed into liquid, solid, and gas by a naked homunculus translator…", as was later written down by the astute caterpillar and future leader of the zoological revolution, Leonor Asphyxiate.

From a crevasse in the rocks, an old horror film is played in triple forward motion, projected onto the back of the copulating human-horse insect by an autistic film buff, whose life's work is splicing together all sex acts committed on celluloid into the one grand *Film to End All Films*. The traitorous actors murmured to anyone that would listen that "…everything is erotic, that everything is sexual. That disease is the love of two alien kinds of creatures for each other." The film cuts suddenly to a scene of a donkey humping an ape amidst a swelling musical crescendo.

Mycobacterium leprae.

The men of the community collectively drop their pants and fondle their erections with both hands.

Yes friends, this is what is often referred to by the crudely mannered as the "Circle Jerk."

This mystical melding of fluids, this golden transmutation much maligned. The Sacred Circle of all occultists and optometrists combined. The women, still gaseous, sweep into the urinary meatus and expand the internals until those male bodies go **POP**. Misguided androcentrism, eternally dispelled in a massive sprouting of red tea and blue-veined flowers.

Meanwhile, the white horse and her boy are letting loose bags of brownish wet fur from the tips of their much enlarged and rapidly changing sexual organs. Undoubtedly, the OR-GANIFICATION, of which has been so often prophesied, is on the cusp of its erotic rupture. A stream of rainbow-tinted sperm shoots into the combined agnus-vanunia hybrid ingrowing on the left hip of the ecstatic boy, who is rapidly transforming into a newly formed organism represented mathematically as:

$$\{[man/(girl + boy) - woman] \times (suitcase - insect)\}/0 = [(woman - woman) \times (-23)]/0 = [0 \times (-23)]/0 = 0/0 = \infty$$

Which we will now simply refer to as "Suitcase."

Suitcase lets out a cry of painful joy, and bites down into the neck of the fluffy horse. It bites down very, very hard. The horse's head falls off and sprouts little spidery legs. It then scampers off into the desert to "find itself" and maybe enjoy a few erotic adventures of its own with some willing cacti or provocatively displayed lizard. Suitcase and Horse, now headless, lay satiated and happy, giving each other mischievous and embarrassed looks. Suitcase wraps itself up in its sticky, fluidic *kethoneth passim*, its spermatozoid coat of many colors, and says, "That was quite a fuck…"

"Oh, just wait till you see my old kink chest!" quips the massive, bloody wound at the end of Horse's quivering nape.

But, to be completely honest, there is no longer any Horse or Suitcase existing at all—merely an unending muscle tremor, dwelling in the rocks and stones, bouncing around contentedly until that dimly perceived and mythologized epoch when cosmos swallows sparrow.

At the Butcher Shop

at the butcher shop
our meat is growing mushrooms
is bleeding out chanterelle
we are the butcher's cast off
we are bovine & blue
today our meat dresses in pattern of light
yes today meat scandalously believes itself
the bright arachnid roadway
meat points to the ancient carvings
along its red flesh
meat is coughing, smiling
butcher brings down his knife
& his head is oval
is axolotl salamander & tardigrade
butcher slices meat's sister in two
but butcher is also blacksmith
on seeing this
meat prepares a speech for us
although he doesn't say it
& at the door of the shop
beneath the rump of our crimson hero
a little cobblestone passageway
is playing at being urban labyrinth

at being metropolitan pied piper
and leads, misleads all comers
into a pinky ocean of toe
while a beach is growing beneath spine
a Parisian ventriloquist
my friend
recalibrate your dreamtime
for the meat maggots are singing a tune
an eulogy for the arrival
of the darkfaced porcupine
from deep within the body of this body
this fragile cowself, this false meat
a main attraction now formulating
a white mold spreading
this slab of calf meat
has opened itself to transference
has spread dripping legs wide
for the universe to penetrate
the sexseed to be dropped in
shall be covered in fur
& in some unrelated elsewheres
suddenly & inexplicably
a meteor grows branches & defecates

Belly Mundus

"Onaka no naka de imomushi umareru"
- words of the Japanese schoolgirl, transfixed (Organ, 1996)

The camera pans in. We are looking down on a wet, Edenic sort of planet, a very lush and rotting place, and we are overwhelmed by an atmosphere of sweat and slime and semen and death. The place looks so warm and so virginal through the view screen that if you look closely, you may notice a few of our tiny intrepid male astronauts below sporting colossal erections. They turn away from their mates shamefully, avoiding eye contact and attempting to shift the material of their oh-so-tight space suits to hide their bulges. Being just a passing death-thought in the mind of an eighteenth-century jellyfish, you may not immediately recall that quite a lot of disgust is piled onto humans of the plant-sexual persuasion these days, and that it is currently illegal in four galaxies. In our viewscreen, a few of these unfortunate fellows break off from the main deck and wistfully relieve themselves inside their cold, steel hibernation cribs. Yikes, but in their excitement they forgot napkin or rag! Oh well. It's been a few years since they've seen anything but the eternal void of deep space, after all, so you can't really blame them. Just clean up after yourselves, please – it's all that we ask.

This campy Sci-fi flick is starting to feel a bit boring now. You yawn and hit fast-forward while thinking vaguely of steak and cream of mushroom soup. A bird's-eye view suddenly appears on screen; you press play and look down on an unnatural clearing in the center of the jungle. In the clearing sits a massive, pinkish mound of undifferentiated and voluptuous flesh, rising and falling rhythmically. If you had to guess, it looks around three stories high. We will call this new creature the "Belly Mundus." A few coarse black hairs grow out of it, some friendlier fur fellows congregating in pubic patches while the other, less social hairs grow off by themselves in world-weary loneliness. At the very top is a cute, spiraling hole that reaches down into the object's center, similar in many respects to a human's belly button. You wonder if this is how it feeds. And if it is an omnivore or a carnivore? Oh distractible Jellyfish, you really must desist with those systematizing questions! Here I am trying my absolute best not to write zoological textbooks for the converted, while you are sitting pretty and endlessly distracting me with your banal, taxidermic echos and pontificating oceanics! I'll skip ahead a few more scenes just to spite you.

Many animals are gathered at the foot of the Belly Mundus in various stages of distress and euphoric pleasure. Our astronauts are there too, covered in bruises, holes, and multicolored pus. Some are sporting great big blissed-out smiles while others look drained dead and empty. They came across old Belly Mundus a few months ago, you see.

Oh god, it is no use, I guess must write…

THE LIFE CYCLE OF THE BELLY MUNDUS

From what we can discern, the Belly Mundus is a large flesh creature that either landed on the Edenic planet in order to infect it, or is an evolutionary descendent of an as-yet-undiscovered native habitat line. No one knows how it initially spouts, *it just does*. It starts small: a little baby tumor snuggly fitted onto the back of some recently deceased plant or animal carcass in the deep jungle. It sucks up any black beetles unlucky enough to walk across its belly button during the first year of its life, but after that, no feeding has ever been recorded. It expands slowly. It overtakes and kills the surrounding plants until it has reached its preferred size and then it stops. At this point, a collection of uncomfortable-looking red pustules grow and spread along the lower half of its heaving body, and a heavy green and red liquid seeps from the wounds. Approximately 20-30 stingers then push their way out from the sores, they are cruel-looking little bastards with very sharp ends. When I first saw these things, I had vaguely thought of them as some sort of erotic wasp-inspired torture devices. They gave me the uncomfortable feeling that I had stumbled upon someone's deeply private fetish world, that I had seen a *very secret thing*, perhaps dreamed up by some resentful hermit over the course of a very long and painful celibacy amongst goats. Darkly whimsical stinger blueprints furtively written down on moldy and semen-stained parchments, later to be mythically forged by the patron saint of all sadists as his final act of appreciation, and forever after consecrated in the blood and feces of all poetically inclined deviants... But I digress as to my original impressions.

According to my observations, these unpleasant stingers secrete a powerfully addictive venom with a rather unique cornucopia of mental effects, and all mammalians of this planet are irresistibly drawn to it. In order to better explain its behavior I will now tell you a tale of one such relatively routine encounter that I witnessed.

Billy is a young deer. He is newly independent and living the good life. While walking about, Billy smells a sweet smell in the forest air; it reminds him of his dear old mother's holiday baking. A fresh cake, or maybe an apple pie! Actually, the smell is merely a pheromone lure secreted by the Belly Mundus, but our plucky hero is a fool. Billy runs in the direction of the smell, growing very, very hungry. He reaches the source, no pie in sight! Oh well, but... Suddenly he sees the big flesh mound and the suggestively drooping stinger. It is just hanging there, swishing about and trembling a bit, almost as if it were saying, "Come hither my sweetness, my love. I am a nice, soft, warm hole to hide in. I am a place to call home... "

The deer shyly walks over to the stinger. He is blushing awkwardly. His brain is in a fog; he can't really think straight. He feels very cozy near the Mundus, but... There is something missing... He could feel even nicer somehow... He sees the stinger and bats his eyelashes at it. An unexplainably powerful, utterly irrational urge overtakes his thoughts. He turns his body around and slowly backs up towards the protruding stinger. It gives him a little jerking upwards movement, a little "hop" of anticipation. With quivering excitement, he lodges the sharp point deep inside his flesh. He feels a majestic wave of euphoria wash over him—what is this marvelous feeling!? He pulls his electrified body out and then forcefully penetrates himself with it again. Wow! He likes it. A lot. Inside his body, little packets of drug-laced sperm swim around, clinging here and there. Some will take root, some won't. In any case, he spends all of his days now at the foot of the Belly Mundus, alternating between moments of blissful erotic frenzy and moments spent in a sleepily incoherent fog. The sperm contains a small amount of nourishment too, so he doesn't completely starve. He must be kept barely alive; he has a purpose now. Bloody punctures and bruises cover his slowly fading body. Wait now—what's that little growth over there, under the left leg? A little bulbous flesh egg has formed! Some time passes. He doesn't inject or move around a whole lot these days. The tumor egg is so heavy that it makes it hard to move, and the injected semen is made up of some kind of new chemical that his body is unable to break down. The stuff is still swimming around inside him, clinging wildly to every squishy soft organ and extracellular lover that crosses its path. This stubbornly indestructible semen is now causing him to hallucinate wildly. He sees the world completely covered in yarn; he sees detached pupils and old bones making earth-shattering speeches to cheering crowds and scantily clad corneas. He sees all the colors of the rainbow speaking to him, whispering sweet promises of a future bliss in all his sensory organs, if he would only sweetly disintegrate for them.

"Become sand, become silica," they murmur, then purr together suggestively. He obliges. From the egg bursts forth a dripping, screaming, furless caterpillar, a frightened new animal mercilessly thrown into this existence at the exact same moment that that the old deer vehicle has expired. It looks about the same length and thickness as my arm and the fanciful family doctor weighs it in at a hefty 38 pounds. The caterpillar's skin is pink and pleasantly loose like a hairless cat or a naked mole rat.

You want to play with it too, don't you? To squeeze its skin, to pinch it? Too bad, this is just a story.

Fanciful family doctor then goes on to plant some rather hard and manly pats on the backs of all those unfortunate enough to be present whilst shouting, "Congratulations, champ, it's a girl!" It slowly crawls out into the forest, living for a hundred years and feasting mostly on dead birds. It never has any children. No one yet knows why the Belly Mundus creates these pink caterpillars or anything else, but we know that they must have something to do with the other Belly Mundus that are showing up on the other continents.

Here ends my explanation of the life cycle of the Belly Mundus. Please don't ask me for any more of the zoological details, you will be utterly bored and have only yourself to blame.

So anyway, the astronauts exploring this Eden look-alike planet noticed a pleasant gingerbread smell hovering in the air, which couldn't help but remind them all of the good ol' times with grandma, and they were soon led to the towering Belly Mundus. They were extremely confused by it, but like all mammals, they quickly fell into the old routine of eroticinjection-euphoria-foggybrain-eroticinjection-hallucination and so on and so on. Something about these pliable new human bodies pleased the Belly Mundus much more than its usual meat vehicles. It found a new way in which to keep them alive from birth to birth. A hazy month of procreation and pain quickly passed by and the men now had numerous half-open and poorly healed birth holes crisscrossing their tired and battered bodies. They had given birth to caterpillar twins, to caterpillar quadruplets, some had even given birth to caterpillar quintuplets! This went on for quite some time and the caterpillar babies had become so numerous that they had even started building claustrophobic little caterpillar civilizations and would soon be discovering cannibalism. The Long Haired Man, however, had had a long string of unsuccessful births. This the Belly Mundus attributed to the poisoned purple berries, which he could not stop himself from gorging on whenever he was not laying around in states of complete euphoric immobility. He came from a long line of noble mushroom hunters back on earth; it was in his blood to forage and he just wouldn't listen to reason.

Belly Mundus had said, "Stop."

Long Haired Man had replied, "No."

It was your typical toxic relationship. Eventually this weird emotional back and forth caused the Belly Mundus' glands to manufacture and secrete a special neurotoxic subhealing substance into the next sperm package it deposited in the troublesome Long Haired Man's body, causing a very painful allergic shock. This new, chemically enriched semen was freshly sentient, but it was not at all organized. It felt a bit lost and unprepared, mixing and mingling with all the wise old bronchial arteries and well-read lymphatic capillaries. It felt like it would much rather be off playing freak at the circus, or fucking a termite colony. But it had a job to do, so it did it. It impregnated the Long Haired Man's left baby toe. A more experienced sperm would have known immediately that this was the absolute worse place to impregnate, but more experienced sperm it was not. In the beginning, this new fetus looked just like all the other Mundus babies, but once a few more of those hazy and delirious days had passed by, the tricky little growth could be seen coalescing into a surprisingly unexpected yet very familiar shape. This was no caterpillar child to be sure, but could it really be a human fetus? Well, we soon found out. The pink pod burst open on the 7th of July, 2178. On that same day, and with no discernable connection between the two events, the civilized caterpillars began cocooning en masse.

There is large mountain of pus, blood, and uterine crustaceans at the foot of the old Belly Mundus. Offal of every conceivable shape and hue vibrates prettily above this long anticipated thing. Look a bit closer and you will see the violently expelled human father's organs, appearing now almost gold and shimmering beneath the light of the waxing triplicate moons. The deceased body of the Long Haired Man lies next to the mound. Time of death: 11:15. Good riddance. Some shivering and jerky movements are seen within the pile. The new creature is panicked and suffocating—it strains to get itself out of the sticky afterbirth. It gives a violent thrust forward, breaks through and is triumphant. It looks up at the sky and opens its mouth very wide.

Noble voyeurs, we listen together with eager expectations of a primal howl, and yet there is none—only silence. There will be no placentophagy occurring today. There will be no mother and no father. We observe this sublimely moist being with wide-open eyes, as it stares resentfully at its supremely perfected form. Who is this new man now standing before us, this exquisite faucet of erotic slime left carelessly dripping and warm for all eternity?

The creature gives the universe a hungry smile, or perhaps a distorted grimace, and it turns and faces us in the mud. It has no eyes and no nose. It has no fingernails and no toes. It has no organs.

The Enigma of the Pit

Our next story takes place near the village of Montignac, in that very famous hole in the earth.

The place with all the cave paintings, you ask?

With the bison 'an stuff?

Yeah kid, you've got it. The exact one.

With that weird painting of a dead half-bird, half-man thing and a weiner next to a buffalo? With all the guts out and stuff?

Kid, now you are just showing off. Please just shut up.

The following account is a rather obscene wet dream from the rocky hive mind of that notoriously perverse cavern-organism, that dirty ol' Lascaux, which was recorded recently via geological dream-suction device. Harvested by a team of Scientific Eroticists without his express consent, and likely of extreme embarrassment to him, we will relay it to you today with an eye for sexual, educational, and moral guidance.

You may now put on your VR helmets.

—

Dream #1

Lost for centuries in a nebulous haze of dark ennui, the Lascaux Cave Mind becomes suddenly excited. His cold cavern skin has felt the sudden touch of a warm animal's flesh, a sensation he'd almost forgotten. A very tight, shamefully bare, distinctly feminine rump has dropped itself down onto his grey subterranean floor.

Oh my!

A delicate Victorian damsel, all covered in lace!

And without any knickers!

He inspects her human mindform and finds within it the beautiful imprint of the name "Collette Junebug." This is her special spirit-name, skillfully tattooed on pumping ethertube walls at birth by some artistically minded nothingforms, the letter lines even written in rare and elegant octopus inks...

Oh, Sweet Collette!

Lascaux Mind is now beside himself with anticipation. He grips his impressively erect stalactites and fondles himself appreciatively. His stiff stone body begins to moisten and to drip...

Collette takes out a blood-stained package from her little green satchel and places it on the floor. Slowly, she unfolds the wet papers, revealing an obscene pile of bright red offal. A motley collection of butcher leftovers, picked up from the town nearby. The pile of meat glows marvelously, spitting out a strange crimson light.

—and its luminous salvia seeps into the eminence of stone
Soaking up Body Form, spreading like bubonic,
She's been caught skinny-dipping in his dead labyrinths,
caught decaying and defiling him
Breaking him down and reforming him—
Changing that deep old darkness of Lascaux
Making him Technicolor-soft, deep fissures goofily vibrant.
He is looking just like an ecstatic cow on milk day.

Collette takes the slippery meat in her hand, and holds it up in appreciation, licentiously enjoying its pleasant weight on her cupped palm, losing herself in reveries of its sweet tactility. *A bit of foreplay perhaps?* Lascaux feels, or perhaps imagines, that the temperature inside the cave is steeply rising. Collette runs the meat across her face ever so lightly, leaving behind a tiny little blood trail. A red butcher's kiss. She gives it a little kiss back, giggles sheepishly, and then moves the meat down towards her lower half. A pause of anticipation, a promiscuous smile— And the two lovers are joined... She presses the meat-man down firmly and with care. She rubs the bloody fluids and smaller lumps inside the thick tangle of her flamboyant pubic mound. She then grips the larger fragments and pushes them deep inside her passionate and greedy hole. Inside both holes in fact—for the anus is hungry, too!

Lascaux is overwhelmed at the sight, he thinks to himself, "Oh, Collette! This honeyed reunion in your flesh, this sweet mingling of entrails and of skinned toe...you are the carrion festival of Bacchus personified! That old cosmic hullabaloo!" Lascaux has always been a rather tiresome classicist, truth be told... Collette's body is now arched and jerking with euphoria. Her clitoris is expertly stimulated by a fast-evolving aggregation of tiny tumor children—completely surpassing the world's top orgasm score and breaking the mindbody sex barrier for the first time in recorded history. The shockwaves of Collette's marvelous orgasm cause the systemic destruction and liquidation of civilization in the outside world. Happy sinkhole parades break out across all seven continents, and the continents themselves shift into the shape of an erect phallus, dissolving all previous nation-state boundaries. America is now merely an undifferentiated patch of foreskin on the left side of the cock, and Canada is a stray pubic hair. Yes, the hunter-gatherer way of life is all that's left for us now. No bosses, no phones. No suburban *Little House on the Prairie*. Deal with it.

Lascaux's stalactite phalli-system suddenly reaches its dramatic climax, ejaculating a soft blanket of white mold across the cavern floor. A supple fungal bed to please his new animal lover...

Dream #2

We open with an energetic, black and white montage full of cosmopolitan clichés. Quick shots of feet hitting pavement, the unpleasant sound of a car honking. Some artful closeups of hurried businessmen rushing along the sidewalk, peppered with the occasional crosscut to an aging proletariat street sweeper for some added grit and socially conscious realism. The disjointed street sounds join together and begin to take on a musical rhythm. The intro ends abruptly and we now see a title screen and a cast of players (none of which is really important). The real action begins:

A bird-faced man is seen walking down a crowded city street. Is this Paris, maybe, or Chicago? *Obviously Lascaux's subconscious doesn't really know the difference.* Our hero walks along happily, tipping his hat to a passing deerman while humming the tune to an old Busby Berkeley musical number. He spies a large fountain up ahead, and looks with confused awe at the strange marble creature towering above its wishing-coin saturated waters. Ah, he remembers this now—the statue of the Great Bison Lord! It had been erected on this spot thousands of years ago by some Paleolithic tribe well versed in sadism, a monument to their strange Ero-Death cosmology. The sacrificial bones of their tortured priests had been found here in droves, hidden just a few meters below the city's whitewashed, modern skin. Another repressed dirty little secret in the heart of our charming city, an episode best left forgotten. They'd found severed arms and legs mostly, but never any intact skeletal frames. Or at least that's what he'd read about it in that French book by Georgie B. But you could never really trust a scholar, now could you?

"It's probably all a load of crap," thought Birdman. "A big stinky pile."

(Our hero Birdman was a born skeptic.)

The sneaky linguists had even coined a new name for the Bison statue, calling it "That Debased Erotonigma." The birdman preferred to call it by the simpler name, "Great Bison Lord," though. He wouldn't be caught dead being a pretentious word-fop like those university types in the uptown hives. He was a real no-nonsense kind of guy.

Today, however, a strange new feeling crept over him in the presence of the statue. His body began to react in uncommon ways—ways he had no reference point for, and no defense against. Was this new feeling even possible? An arousal to the inanimate? A love, even? Those big, hairy stone legs rearing up in cataclysmic rage, those extravagant entrails waving...

"What a dish!" Birdman thought to himself.

His purple penis ripped itself out from a centuries-long blue jean imprisonment, dispelling a cloud of uncomfortable American fabrics. A neighboring commune of pigeons even began to sing the Internationale, pausing their rooftop frolicking in order to show solidarity with our newly freed Birdman... A colony of surprised ant squatters then suddenly appeared at the tip of his cock, shooting out from his newly exposed urethral hole and running off down the nearest rat-filled alleyway. They'd been living in the birdman's shaft rent-free for quite some time, thanks to a helpful tip from the sympathetic scrotum. *Time to regroup and find another orifice,* they think, *or (even better!), to rekindle the old guerrilla tactics and start fun-filled insectoid insurrection against those monolithic pesticide death-makers!*

A young and rather likable ant kid named Joey Strumma gives his friends a rousing antipesticidal speech, boldly concluding, "The future is unwritten! Hail Satan and down with all pesticidal punks!"

Birdman, however, only has eyes for the Great Bison Lord. Such a provocative stone-thing, such a colossal hunk! He sees now the absurdity of all the old dichotomies, of those illusory myths of contradiction—the living set against the unliving, the flesh set against the stone… They are united under the spectral sign of his erotic geographies, of his alembic signifiers. His human body has turned 30 today, but his umbilical cord has only just now been cut, irreversibly severed in his mad love for the diabolic Bison-Form. He is the loose body drifting in the house of the dead, a wide-eyed foreigner in Xibalba. He walks towards the statue, holding his penis with his right hand. He squawks at it with his bird beak and gives it a confusing sad-happy smile. The he lets himself have a few casual strokes. He steps in a circle around the Bison, waving his human arms up and down and stamping his feet. A kind of archetypal bird-brain courtship memory seems to be taking over his body, bubbling up from the depths. An ancient birdy sex recipe! These shocking directives had been long ago dreamwritten onto the wall of the collective birdconsious by a gang of feathery perverts and Casanovas, their empty aerosol spray cans still left to rust across the avian mindfloor… Birdman walks up to the statue, gently touching it with his beak. He nibbles sweetly at its frozen, exposed intestines, and the statue begins to purr with rage. It begins to regain its color. Our hero whispers to the statue, confiding to it in the language of the birds. He sticks his left leg up in the air and then slams it back down again, then repeats this with the opposite leg. His erect phallus shakes itself in merry bounce with each impact. Great Bison Lord's face goes red at the sight. We aren't really sure if he is angry now or just shy? Perhaps too many years have passed since his last sexual partner, and he is not sure what to do next? More unconscious rituals pass themselves through the Birdman's trancing puppet body. His purple penis gives out a long litany of erotic provocations, too. Eventually the Great Bison Lord is fully colorized. He is now very smelly and covered with coarse brown hair. *Just like a real bison, kids!* The falling intestines lift up inside him, drop down, and then lift up again. The mythical moment of wounding played out forever on a cruel, unending, red loop. Birdman sees and understands. This ritual demands one action, and one action only. He knows where he must penetrate his Bison-Lover. He climbs up onto the side of the Bison Lord, and takes his thick purple penis in hand.

He whispers to the universe, he tells it a secret: *"Become Pansexual Jelly."*

And then—

Birdman thrusts his sex deep inside the mouth of that ever-opening, ever-closing cosmic wound, expelling a flood of warm semen into the expectant nothingness. Filling it, finally.

And in the Good Book of the traveling monk, this passage is now writing itself:

"This morning, I looked out into the cosmos with the aid of my God Telescope, naively expecting all the usual celestial and satanic banalities. Imagine my horrified surprise when I observed that that troublesome old void had transformed itself overnight, becoming a vast, milky ocean of seminal white…It's walls are now irreversibly pollinated, it smells obscenely of sex, and it is noticeably with child. Oh, the debauchery!"

Bison Lord screams out in violent rage at the moment of sexual consummation, convulsing wildly and knocking Birdman away from his tender slit. Sharp hooves stamp down onto the fallen Birdman's back, and our hero is soon impaled though the chest by the unyielding horn of the Great Bison.

And yet, Birdman's penis remains erect.

He is our hero.

Oedema of Head

if enough people in this city start practicing animism
if enough people start talking to bricks
caressing concrete
humping glass
yes if enough people start licking streetlamp
then
i promise you
this old city will gain back its flesh
will jump up
smile & shout
"i'm a real boy!"
the pinocchio-scraper shall rise up
casting away the doubters
leaving behind little eggy piles
of sticky who-knows-what
across the moaning pavements
& aggravating the wistful commuters
who
like Job
shall shake their miserablist fists to the architectural heavens
& cry mournfully
yes
this municipal deadspace

this vampiric metal
shall soon fill with divine dream-breath
& inky eros shall gain dominion
it will happen
on some unremarkable day
without any warning
mr. iron & mrs. plastic
so sad & unresponsive
for long eons
shall turn suddenly a reddish-blue
& do an awkward pee-pee dance
& their shit & their piss shall drop from a great height
dirtying the fur of the bourgeoisie
this shining meat metropolis on the hill
shall require very skilled gynecologists
hematologists
ophthalmologists
in fact
this "cityscape fleshoid prophecy" from which I now recite?
it is actually *realtime divination*
FOR THE FLESHTOWN
OF THE FUTURE
IS ALREADY HERE
but I see that skeptical eyebrow raise
on blackened insect forehead
I see how it has detached itself
fluttering around the cold room
& fucking moth & fucking beetle

& birthing witty little scholar-forms
yes yes don't even try to hide it
you damn dirty punk
but despite all this
despite your pleasuredome antics
in the crotch of the metamodern
yes & despite your recent shenanigans
with that sleazy mermaid pornographer
despite it all
THE UNDERCITY LIVES
& it is all quite irreversible my friend
though it is presently engaged
on the reptilian astral plane
& so is still unseen by most
& is not taking any reservations
so stop trying so hard
stop pushing & straining
like that
you're going to hurt yourself
all in good time etc. etc.
yes even a spirit needs a laxative sometimes
ah but truly
this is the longed for legendtime
this is aeon of "HUMAN X"
yes
the worldform is feeling quite soft today
for its cityfur has started growing out
& my shiny little egregore

has been bathed with a spongebath of silver
yes truly
this must be the oedema of the head

Expressing the Milk

We looked out onto a vast ocean of milk. Swarms of over-sexed barnacles have lactated so profusely in recent years that the old familiar salt water has been consumed, lost under per-petually renewing torrents of thick mammary whiteness. The few fish that survive have regressed back to childhood, suckling wildly at the surrounding milk in between desperate cries of "wah-wah." The climate changes of the last century have eroti-cally stimulated some creatures at the expense of others.

An albino humanoid drifts up from the deep, parting the floating islands of curdled milk and deliriously giggling fish-es. He sniffs curiously at the sourness hanging in the air, takes one hesitant step forward and then another. His dripping white skin seems very thick, and is covered with thousands of tiny lit-tle bumps. It looks exactly like the flesh of some newly plucked, beheaded, and blood-drained chicken, a freshly mangled casu-alty of pastoral life, artfully displayed. A few parasitic nipples grow on the edges of his distended ear lobes, but the chest is bare. He is not milk producing at this time.

The albino touches ground below the surface and con-tinues to wade towards us through the whiteness. As the sur-rounding milk becomes lower, we can't help but notice a very large, very extravagant phallus dangling about heavily from his completely hairless crotch. He reaches the beach and shakes himself off like a wet dog. He sinks his feet into the hot sand and gives us a big, *shit-eating* grin – whatever that is. Down un-derneath the wet sand, he spreads his supple toes out wide and then closes them. He just loves the feeling of gooey little things coming in between his toes. A strong bodily urge to defecate teases at his sphincter. This is a completely new sensation for the albino, and he stubbornly ignores it. His anguished gut pleads for mercy but it is of no use, he won't give in—in fact, he could hold it for years if he wanted to! Consequently, a salmonella-birthed, psi-power decay-surge floods hydrogen sulfide packets into all his chicken pores, causing a new outbreak of Vaseline vibrations on his arm. He feels invincible.

Elsewhere...

The guillotine sits on the beach, primed and nearly ready for the next milkman. (*Him?*)

Oh ancient murder machine, sitting there so luminous and infinite beneath the blinding lights of the apexed noonday sun, what treasures will you bring today?!Your blade so freshly polished—so exciting!

The Lilliputian caretakers franticly climb about on the deranged object, scrubbing the sacred metal and double-checking its aging wooden surfaces for freshly gnawed termite holes. These tiny workers must be no more than a pinky finger's length—what exotic little men! Some seem much less humanoid than their fellows: we see a few pinchers and scaly growths covering their extremities. This should be of no surprise, for it is well documented in the literature that Lilliputians breed openly with insect, mouse, and worm. Live birth and egg-laying are practiced freely and interchangeably among them, and on rare occasions, bee pollination via ear canal has even been observed. The busy little creatures have finished their daily rounds and call out to the silent albino man from the sea. He hears their pleasant summons and after a bit of thought, decides that he will in fact approach this alluringly depraved guillotine-thing. The Lilliputians scramble to their designated operation nests, then motion for him to climb up and place his head on the freshly polished altar.

"What luck!" they think. "He certainly looks much fresher than the previous milkmen. No more failed batches! At least not for now."

The albino milkman takes a long and wistful look at this beckoning new head-hole. Previously only dead weight to him, the excited meat column between his legs suddenly pulls itself up from the sand it had been dragging in and becomes as hard and erect as an overwatered topiary. He feels confused by his very first erection. He doesn't understand it at all. He thinks, "What the hell is this?" It is, after all, the very first milkman erection to occur in the long history of his flesh, and we are all feeling pretty surprised and excited about it, too. *My dear milk-man phallus, you sweetly sublime originator of all future erections on this planet, we salute you!* A transcendent new festival will forever after mark this day. It will be dream-drenched and erotic-communal, a celebration completely untouched by dead religion or stale saints. Merry Phallomas!

The albino milkman proceeds. The air near the machine is thick with phantom smells of rotten fruit. He climbs the ramp and finds the platform unpleasantly hot, and his delicate white feet recoil in pain. Baby toes tell of burning embers underneath, but his eyes can't see a damn thing; it's just normal wood as far as he can tell. He moves forward, trying his best to ignore the invisible sensations. He places the head of the holy phallus inside the soft, circular throne, thrusting, penetrating deeply into its etheric hymen. Then he stands, his face in a silent howl, bulging and expectant.

The command is given and the blade drops.

A storm of white milk and cream tar splash violently from the newly severed tip, covering all of the Lilliputians. Antago-nistic colors and opposing tactilities—these contrarian forms now mix and mingle in viscous, diabetic unifications – a blanket of happy revulsion now ready to moisturize an entire world. At the moment of slicing, the albino milkman's repressed and long suffering colon also lets forth a parallel, unexpected, deluge, consisting of his long-suffering and unjustly imprisoned feces—an event perhaps even eclipsing the Tar-Milk eruption, if weighed on a hydraulic Blavatsky scale of uterine-psychological destructive forces. The smell is intense. Surprised Lilliputians gag and cover their noses; a few climb down from the guillotine and regurgitate lunch.

Ah, but that's not all! The cavernous wound on the phallus seems to grow and to expand after its decapitation. We can gaze deep into the lacerated abyss but see absolutely nothing. Nada. Zilch. Just a hint of rich perfumes. Suddenly a blurred flash of color is fired from deep inside, falling a few feet behind us. Closer inspection reveals a moving mountain of fruit-flavored candy drops. Every possible color on the spectrum (and a few more besides!) is represented here. The candies are sporting cute baby insect feet on their undersides. They move about aimlessly and look like chewable mounds of ladybugs. A few Lilliputians bag a candy bug or two to take home to hungry families. This sugary sweet feast will be a fitting way to celebrate the newly coined Phallomas holiday, they muse. Another whooshing sound breaks from the void, and a second rainbow flash drops dead nearby. Look there—a lively collection of multicolored flowers and plump purple eggplants! *My, my, we'll all be feasting for weeks!* We collect the vegetables and flowers and place them inside the antique wicker baskets appearing in the sand. The obscene wound at the end of the prick then spits out its third and final treasure, its cheerful parting gift before the evaporation. The triumphant ejaculation sails high above us as the milkman's flesh turns spectral and goes dark. The heavy load descends, meeting the ground in forceful impact. Clouds of sand mask our vision and stifle our breaths, but soon it disperses.

The objects now sitting before us?
Millions upon millions of greasy, well-loved crayons.

An Afternoon Among
Miniatures

Part 1: rationalizations

As a kid I often played with my sister's dollhouse. It was a tall Victorian affair which had been passed down through the family and hand-built by my great-grandfather. Many dreamy afternoons were spent imagining my life lived among tiny chairs, eating tiny food, perhaps even cohabiting in this blue mansion together with my tiny wife. We'd rub our naked bodies together on tiny little beds, and eventually she'd defecate some tiny children, as I continued in my belief that babies were expelled via anus until the age of 10 or 11.

Around this time, I was also exposed to a friend's magnificent railroad diorama in the basement of his house, which his grandfather had spent years building for him. After seeing this, my father and I became obsessed with building a miniature rail-world of our own. I helped him as he created the tiny towns and weirdly textured landscapes, watched as he painted and glued the idealized American shops. Places like Bob's Grocery, or Bill's Auto Shop. Places like Sally's Diner. I was transfixed by it all, watching as the little train circled endlessly round this idyllic place inhabited by invisible peoples. Yes, and why the complete absence of living forms? Perhaps others have small figurines or dolls which they integrate into these sets, but I don't think mine ever did. It was like watching an empty stage set, waiting for its lead actor to take the stage. Me? Or perhaps the little people existed there already, and one would need only a shift in consciousness to see them, to arrive at the right time, or to utter the words of a secret spell. All those Otaku hobbyists out there obsessively building civilizations in miniature—are they merely the unwitting dupes of faery folk, enchanted worker bees and slaves to the whims of little men?

In the field of eroticism, there exist a few strains of pornography in which the erotic potential of tiny things is being mined. After all, what man among us has not harbored the impossible dream of a cum-covered faery in phallic embrace? And what woman could possibly turn away the advances of a skilled homunculus lover, ardent spelunker of womenkind's deepest vaginal cavern systems? In certain spheres, photographs of debased dolls and figurines are exchanged, their plastic bodies partially covered in the semen of a collector-lover. Unrealizable dreams, half-realized.

Another thought: In many cultures, magic spells are cast using a miniaturized effigy of some kind. Perhaps as a surrealist experiment, I should create a life-like diorama of the entire capitalist world. Instead of sticking it with pins, I would squat awkwardly above it, squeezing out painful cataclysms of liquefied shits onto the obnoxious poppet world, dispelling it into murky brown nonexistence. Irritable bowel syndrome finally put to good use? And would the revolution triumph then?

Part 2: fabrications

A naked boy stands before the water door. The opening's transparent form looks like coiling white flesh in the process of evaporation, like the tightly woven muscles of some recently skinned and albino-filamented Gulliver. The boy readies himself for submersion and passage; he takes the step forward.

The heavy liquid seeps itself into his ears, his nose, into every orifice. He sees almost nothing now but a thick grey fog. There is a feeling here of breathing deeply and being suffocated simultaneously. A feeling of deep winter frosts. A rusty metal hook reaches down inside his mouth and pulls out unnecessary organs and extraneous bacterium. These organs and microorganisms are then released and float away, slowly turning white and hardening. They look just like classroom chalk. A transgender mosquito swims over to the chalky forms, breaking them up into pieces with his elongated feeding tube and thin legs. As they drift away, the boy begins to cry. An ocean-going hedgehog swims over to him, says, "Everything is going to be ok, so don't worry!" It expels a train ticket from its gill and places it in the boy's shivering hands. The sopping wet and barely legible ticket says, "All aboard the organ train! No need for an organ plane! (One admission, expiration at puberty)." The blurred ticket is designed in an art nouveau style and accompanied by elaborately decadent swirls and patterns that call to mind 1920s Paris and cabaret posters. On the back of the ticket, a charming scene of a magnificently sensual female wasp sporting skimpy yet elegant attire, dancing in a vintage nightclub for an audience of well-dressed, roly-poly businessmen smoking expensive cigars. The boy's vision changes, drops, dissociates. His left tear duct burns, and from its corner drips out a molten hot silver liquid and some unidentifiable globular forms which look like oversized poppy seeds. The discharge collects into one shining puddle at his feet and is soon retrofitted and reopened as a new hot spring bath by colonies of pushy white maggots. The smoky nightclub scene continues to engulf him as he stares fixedly, beginning to pass into it and through it. His flesh is transferred like a bit of squeezed fruit from one form of perception to another. Though admittedly he loses some healthy fibers in translation, I still stand by my previous statement that a frequent form molting is advisable, healthy and desired. In fact, my daily regiments of organ tissue juicing have made me feel like an absolutely virile porcupine, and who could complain about that? But back to the boy...

Once he is fully juiced into the darkened nightclub, the roly-poly businessmen all fall over, mysteriously expiring at the sight of his holy arrival. It is time for the crowning of fresh vegetables and liquids, for today is Micropsia Monday! Everything in the world looks off to the boy. The objects feel subtly deranged from their proper scales and visual weights, as though produced by large hands under a magnifying glass. He wonders, is he the unlucky new inhabitant of some Kaiju town scheduled for immediate demolition? Let's hope not, this story has just begun, though it's clear it will end soon. The initial disorientation subsides, and he looks over at the erotically-charged wasp. It is just the two of them in the room now, and he feels like he is the last man on earth. Time to get fruitful, honey! The wasp blows him a kiss and pulls down its lacy dress. It turns toward the wall and gets on all fours, flicking its wings excitedly. With its elongated wasp fingers, it spreads its yellow slit wide. The vagina lips open and close like a fish mouth, convulsing awkwardly in uncontrollable tics. Most wasps of this world are carriers of the genital Tourette's; it can't be helped. Actually, he is starting to feel his own shaft act in a strange manner too, twisting unnaturally and repeating a long string of unintelligible vocal sounds. Is it contagious? He walks toward the stage, and with his arms and feet he tries spreading the wasp's hole even wider. He then sees a conveniently placed collection of bejeweled gynecological objects waiting there by the stage and notices the newly installed silkscreened wall paneling explaining their ritualistic use by ancient cults. He puts the mechanisms into place and for now, the wasp's convulsing seems under control. He peeks inside but sees only stars and the left arm of the Milky Way. *Well, maybe I'll crawl in there when I'm older*, he thinks. "If I crawl in there right now, I might end up on the wrong side of her amorous caterpillar lover or stabbed to death by an obsessed fan club of psychotic pixies, and who could save me then? To be honest the age gap seems a tad inappropriate too, I think I'll pass this time…"

He thanks her for obliging him so readily and throws a few sticky candies inside as a parting gift. He then removes the ceremonial gynecological tools and the vagina closes itself down with a pout and a sigh. *Ugh, cosmic orgasms are so hard won these days*, she muses. *Everyone is just too busy to fuck. Maybe I'd have better luck living in a universe made of slugs. Some eternally moist pleasure world no longer held together by cold, stupid atoms, but with masses of those squirming slimy little beasts leaving cute trails everywhere! It would always be raining there, or at least drizzling, and all salt would be outlawed. I could just sit down and open up my legs anywhere I pleased, just let them work their magic as they crawled over me!* She blushes. The boy decides to walk outside now, confused by the wasp's sudden lack of communication with him and the far-away look in her eyes.

He opens the door and almost gets himself crushed under the wheels of a speeding passenger train. The hair follicles on his body fly off in the ensuing gust of wind, and he now stands before us as bald as a newborn babe (and still naked, too). "Whatever," he thinks, "I don't care a fig about those damn follicles. I've always hated the feel of the slimy shampoo on my head anyhow. Conditioner on the other hand…well, perhaps I'll miss that substance a little. Overall, I think I just prefer a thicker consistency in my liquids."

It is a nice spring day outside so the boy decides to take a stroll. He tips his imaginary hat to the well-dressed moles, moths, and butterflies as they pass. Such a pleasant little city! They trade a few "good days" and "what nice weather we're having" to each other. Carefree young marsupial children ring bells and ride past him on a few thick, awkwardly construct-ed bicycles. It must be admitted that the hands of the creator giants are often too large and clumsy to build on such small scales convincingly. Suddenly a large mantis with an over-stuffed leather suitcase and top hat runs down the street and bumps into the boy, accidentally severing his left arm with his sharp forelegs. The bastard doesn't even apologize! The arm is lodged in the gutter now, it turns an ugly grey and starts growing maggots and dandelions, almost instantaneously. *Well, that's a complete loss*, he thinks. An orange syrupy substance drips down from his fresh wound. Faeries soon rush to his side, hid-den until now inside discarded fruit peels, dead flowers, and the ear canal of one very surprised opossum. Some only as tall as a pinky finger, while others have ballooned to the size of a toddler or even full-grown mini-human. They have long, bloodied teeth and uncommonly enlarged genitals from which he can see a slow ooze of discharge, left to a slow drip like a faucet in winter. A few have the now rather tired and cliché (to us) butterfly wing look, but the more creative of faeries bran-dish wings inspired by the beautiful damselfly or the industri-ous honey bee. Without a doubt, the oddest are those sport-ing the antique yet still rather flashy airplane wings. This new category of retro-airplane Fae being split more-or-less evenly between the biplane and the triplane varieties. A few of the creatures have no wings at all, or just a few stunted and pathet-ic salamander tails attempting to grow out in the gaps between their toes. A parasitic cloud of ghost scholar energies passes through the boy and he finds himself beginning an abrupt ponder. "Perhaps these are the original models on which all subsequent tiny folklore creatures are based? Had some intrep-id Neanderthal scout already passed through this world in the distant past and taken notes? Were these the "Adam Kadmon" of shobijin, the primordial Fae?" His *deep thoughts* continued to run themselves in little circles until the parasitic ghost scholar energy was satiated, leaving him then to drift on down the road in search of fresh prey.

The little creatures are congregating desperately around the rim of the orange molasses puddle dripping from where his arm was. They suck it up through their hollow fangs, acting as though they hadn't eaten for days. A few smaller ones fly up to the boy's open wound, sniffing at it excitedly. These unpleasant fellows waste no time at all and burrow deep inside his body. He screams out, "Ugh, fuck a duck!" His hip jerks side to side like he is trying out a new dance routine and failing miserably. The Fae soon reach his intestines, and he can tell without a shadow of a doubt that they have all his fleshly tummy tubes in between their strong little legs and are squeezing down hard. Everything inside him is feeling so tight now, he hunches over and squeals like a tortured pig. He has never felt pain like this and he is so frightened and so scared, he can't even speak or think anymore; he wants it to stop so desperately. Grasping at anything, he thinks for a moment about praying to God or Kali for relief, but his fingernail seethes with rage at the suggestion and coolly tells him, "I don't eat that bread." Oh no, and the intestine has popped! Out comes the shit wave! It flushes itself out rapidly through repurposed blood vessels and drops itself from the arm hole. Though I can see now that this sly young bowel movement had time enough for a few unscheduled stops along the way and has smeared large amounts of himself onto the skylights and topiaries of the extravagant McMansions owned by a few of the more well-to-do organ groupings. The muffled, whiny voice of a blackened lung is heard crying, "This is scandalous, utterly contemptible! Where are my bronchioli housekeepers? I want a bubble bath! Bodily waste should not, it cannot exist!" This satisfyingly juvenile prank on the part of the excrement was his last statement to the world, before glorious suicide by harsh impact with unyielding concrete slab. His unmoving brown form sits there on the cold sidewalk, looking pancaked and very, very dead. And yet, even in death he is defiant—if you look closely, you will see his fecal tongue sticks out at the world still, stuck forever in a playfully insubordinate death grimace. I have no doubt that future revolutionaries and criminals will one day make pilgrimage to this fecal holy of holies, which they will stand in awe and offer gifts of ripe fruits and salty tears to the divinely dissident brown stain on the sidewalk. Of course, this is assuming that there will be any future at all, and that we won't have all devolved into caterpillar men with no legs by then.

(I wouldn't mind really, but it makes it very hard to travel long distances, you know?)

The boy feels much better now. How refreshing it is to walk this bright city, to feel so buoyant and so emptied! He yells, "I feel like a fluffy pink cloud!" to no one in particular, raising a few grumpy amphibian eyebrows. He realizes suddenly that his last bowel movement was over a week and a half ago. No wonder he'd felt so weighted down! *Those little people must have been quite skilled doctors,* he muses, *for they knew the problem within me even before I did. No doubt they are all extremely well trained in the budding science of Intestology and the fashionable ideologies of Fecalism and Urinophagy, which are so popular among the Pre-K and Elementary School children this year.*

(And of which the boy currently knew absolutely nothing. "A Very Simple, Extremely Straightforward Introduction to Fecalism by TJ Offal" was still collecting dust on his bathroom shelf. After a page or two of the jargon-heavy writing, our hero had started to feel that it was just too stuffy and confusing for his tastes.)

Many teachers had banned the well-meaning TJ Offal's books from schools, the book-collecting mania being so strong this year that outbreaks of violence and child book gangs were becoming commonplace. The nationwide shortage of toilet paper caused by Offal's teachings had put everyone on edge, too.

The boy's thoughts then moved away from the problem of TJ Offal and drifted about for a while, landing on nothing in particular. He reached the end of the sidewalk presently, walked up to the nice overlook and saw the river below. The river was a deep black and had a strangely unnatural, undulating movement to it. He felt disturbed by its presence, but was not sure why. Next to him was a coin operated telescope for sightseeing. He dropped a few coins in and took a closer look. As he peeked in he began to feel sickened again. His mind and even body rejected what he saw. He started to gag and grabbed at his chest painfully, almost covering his telescope in a steamy brown blanket of a previous meal. The river below was not made up by water at all, but by billions of eternally fucking, eternally spawning millipedes. All types were present and accounted for, their bodies claustrophobically smushed into one another. It was impossible to know with any certainty where one millipede ended and the next began. They were all sizes imaginable, too. Some stretched the length of the city, while others were as short as a baby garden snake or snail. The colors of the bodies, however, were always only that same oppressive black lighticide which the boy had first seen and been so repulsed by. *Was this Insectkind's taunting reflection of our deepest spiritual void?*—cruel detritivore pleasures gained in shoving our pudgy, hairy man faces into the rotten cesspools of our own absence of meanings? Perhaps, triumphantly shouting, "No longer shall we consent to be squished, neither by foot nor by flyswatter, you soft bellied swine!"

Insects aren't affected by our "meaning of life" questions, and they don't understand Nietzsche at all. But I guess they know enough to hit us where it hurts.

Well, a bit of time passes by, and the motionless boy slowly becomes desensitized to the crawling horrors. Maybe he even loves them a little, maybe he longs for squirmy piles of them to crawl up from deep in his throat and spill out over his wet lips in sweetly bashful insectoid first kisses, to live out the first ever human-millipede love affair? Or perhaps this is just another case of our swashbuckling hero's trial by torture—painful at first, but leading to an inevitable sense relief and renewed journeying? His intestine certainly seems fine now, anyway.

A strange physical compulsion suddenly fills his body, which his reluctant mind still rejects. His defiant hands pull the body up over the railings and drop him down into the swarm below.

The fall proceeds in gentle slow-motion effect. Minutes pass and the entire city holds its breath as he falls. Finally, the chubby pink butt cheek impacts with the millipede swarm, exploding impressively in a marvelous tactility-form of an enraged, abandoned mattress melted and grafted onto the fading memories of a suck at his mother's breast. He thinks of hot Swiss cheese and swoons. He is carried along with the black mass, and a heaving insect wave soon pushes him down below. He expects immediate suffocation here but finds himself breathing normally. At deeper levels, the atmosphere starts to feel very hot and humid too, like a sticky summer evening in the humid south. Eventually, his submerged body is expelled via spiraling millipede orifice into a dark and cavernous air pocket inside the mass of insects. It is here that King Millipede sits on his metallic throne, surrounded by undulating walls and centipede concubines. He points his staff at the boy and cries, "Hesava amin! Delock in! Aregos delay ar spongecocoon?" The spell takes and the boy's skin hardens and turns a hard, shiny, deep black, which he is completely encased in. Worker ants climb inside his ear hole and whisper to him mischievously, telling him that this magnificent new armor is a disease-cocoon with which he may later storm heaven, that it is a mystical bacteriophage evolved from interiors of inky blackness in order to infect divine flesh with sexually transmitted disease. The angels shall drown in oceans of their own genital discharge, the ants exclaim, and a syphilis-mad God will devour his own infected papules and mucous membranes! The boy agrees to King Millipede's plan, it seems like a pretty amusing joke to him on God. In fact, he's always loved a good prank. He waves goodbye, then jumps back into the moving millipede wall and is carried on down the canal, tickled all the while by tiny millipede arms and giggling uncontrollably. A fork in the path of the river soon comes up, and a cresting wave deposits him back onto solid ground.

He stands up and shakes his body off, dispelling clouds of the black dust and soot which had gathered on his body during his long swim in the black river. He soon succeeds in drying himself and takes a look at the new surroundings. A massive golden superstructure stands before him, dwarfing the surrounding shops and apartments with bombastic luminescence. Built in an overblown Greek revival style, he wonders if this is the city hall or a courthouse of this place. There is an ancient-looking sign posted near the front entrance to the left of the stairs. He walks over to it, hoping to discover this majestic building's true name, but the label merely reads, "Bill's

Auto Shop." Bemused by this new development, he shrugs his shoulders and ascends up the immaculate marble staircase.

On reaching the top of the stairs, he is picked up and raised into the sky by a wrinkled old human hand about thirty times his size. The air rushes by; he feels disoriented and panicked. He worries vainly about his sudden heart palpitations and rubs together his two very tiny, and now very sweaty hands. To calm himself down, he tries some breathing exercises and counts the passing birds, he even tries his hand at a little cloud-bursting. The anxiety soon fades away but he feels so very sad now. He misses that rapidly shrinking miniaturist world of the city below. It had felt like a new home, a promising new fresh start for him, and the animals were all so very nice down there.

(Well, except for that rude mantis!)

He is sucked up past the pink clouds, past the planets and the stars and the old hardening multiverse clusters. Majestic forms shrink to nothingness below his rising feet. He finds himself inside a room with drab grey walls and a cobweb problem. It seems to be someone's musty basement. He hears a model train making its noisy rounds from somewhere behind him, but can't quite place it. He breathes a sigh of relief now, this certainly isn't heaven, and that wrinkled hand certainly isn't God. For a brief moment he'd been worried that he'd been "found out" by that flaccid ol' demiurge, and wouldn't get a chance to try out his fancy new bacteriophage...

The big hand puts the kid's loose skin flaps in between his dirty oil-stained fingernails and holds him up to eye level. Such a familiar face! The boy wonders what his Grandpa is doing here, and why is he so gigantic? Grandpa's weathered face is now completely covering the boy's visual field. A parasitic cloud of drifting ghost artist energies passes through the boy's right nipple and looking at his Grandpa's face he exclaims,

"What lovely planetary landscapes, what amazing textures! Those deeply dredged Martian wrinkle canals and delightfully puffy old flesh mountains...no doubt about it, this is a face with some serious character!" This is all very odd for a boy like him to suddenly utter, but his doddering old Grandpa doesn't notice a thing. The boy then tells his Grandpa all about his exciting new adventures inside the miniaturist realm, though it is a bit murky as to how much of the narrative Grandpa is really able to process. His eyes seem a bit foggy, maybe his cataracts are worsening, or maybe he is just going through the motions and thinking of other things?

Grandpa looks down at him and bellows, "Welcome to the microscopic life, kiddo!"

Cenote

Night passes and I wake from an imageless slumber. I push myself out from my dark water cocoon and climb jerkily up the side of the Sacred Cenote, up towards the sun and its warmth. My worm-like body leaves behind a sticky-sweet residue, and I sense each new step through the six slits of my face, these parallel cuts assigned to a diverse range of sensory organs. I can smell her, she is near—her hide like leather and salmon, insides white and glowing. I pass the mouth of the cenote and slide into the forest. She lets out a low, vibrating hum, letting me know she is ready. Triggered by this hum, my body begins to secrete a textured red honey from my facial slits. We touch under the decaying vegetation and begin to affix our massive prehensile bodies to each other. Her core bright and pulsating, spinning rapidly as our dark liquids seep into each other's heated flesh. Far beneath her third tail, a small patch of hair waits, grows and retracts itself moment by moment. The circular flap near my stomach opens up and my Euclidean organs ooze out onto the forest floor. Her hair stems grow bigger than ever before, wrapping themselves around my deposited innards and pressing them until they burst. From inside, little tumble bugs scurry out and run for the treetops, trailing blackish smells. With my waning strength I pull myself into the folds of her shell and drop the rest of my deflated body onto her center. Poisoned fluids, now dripping from us both, eat our bodies and our thoughts. We drift silently into death.

As the days pass, our decomposing bodies will combine, one sweetly putrid flesh with no differentiation. At the center of this mound two eggs will form, nebulous siblings to repeat the eternal cycle once more.

Me and My Sac Fungi

this year i desire

penetration-infatuation-evolution

via cordyceps

i have submitted my request

to the higher-ups

i have orifice-expelled

some blueprints, plans

my sexualspiritual desire

has even vibrated

into a moist sponge

for all to see

dear friend

look inward and you will notice

these bored monolithic membranes

have all grown sanctuaries

have sprouted out

(via rectal seeding)

five immaculate mycelium conceptions

in other words

the eukaryotes are birthing their exponential harvest

and

the bloodmind says after all,

the bloodmind says yes

oh my

here we are now

here we go

we reader-voyeurs standing together all in a line

humid and breathless on dream balcony

before our virginal eyes—

magnificent gardens jungles oceans

of dreamtumor crop

our subservient flesh

is coming into its own

is finally asserting itself

and has also been withholding from stern old Ego

a recent deluge of embarrassing infection fantasies

Bob yells, "Oh, but we've heard all that before, fiend! The human collapse,
palmistry-divined on citystreetlines!"—then continues his insertion of bio-
luminescent pearls under his glowing foreskin…

yes yes

don't be so conceited

because i've read all that too

but

i've often noticed ms. 'human form' losing herself lately

it's been a woolgathering sort of month for her

spent in secretive image making

her silent evenings pass in erotic thoughtfilm

playing pictures of alien or barbarian invasion

doesn't matter which

pictures of flesh programming rewrites

of debased nucleotides with loose morals

and she wants the saliva sac to ejaculate out
this bluedyed request as soon as possible
this cavern call
for a sanctified sacred pain
for a microscopic possession
for each and every fungus running wild
deep down inside us
a parasitic new alien lover
no exorcist will ever cast out
oh sweet cordyceps
dissolve me
succulate me
play the role of my platonic half this spring
and grow from my head like a crown
editors note:
you may notice
this fashionable new form of fungal body modification
will soon be catching on
in all the right places
—next fall

A Hurried Exposé on Traditional Intestinal Theatre by Dionysus Destructo and His Pals

My name is Dionysus Destructo. My parents were pencil-birthed inside the panels of a trashy '60s comic book series, and I received this rather awkward name thanks to them. I was just another unwanted byproduct of their failed shrink ray experiments. Later, during my university days, I succeeded in breaking the fourth wall, and here I am, and I never looked back. After receiving my degree, I got hired on as a journalist for Entrails Monthly, which is why I sit here today, impatiently waiting for this play to start. My obnoxiously hardboiled, chest-hair-expectorating boss had handed me a sweat-stained flyer for a local performance of "Traditional Intestinal Theatre" last Thursday, and demanded the 2000-word write-up by Monday, his gruff voice dripping with veiled job-security threats and masculine ectoplasm. It's Saturday evening now and the show is about to begin.

The performance takes place inside the walls of a repurposed old church – tall ceilings, stained glass. It seems like it's only used for musical performances these days. The pews have all been removed and replaced with rickety bleachers, like the kind you'd see in a high school gymnasium.

The lights go dim around us, and a deep silence descends onto the room, cutting out and dissolving our speech and active thoughts. Some sort of spiritual-surgical operation is being performed on us with phantom-bloodied knives from hidden atmospheres, from high up altitudes, with the delightfully sweet feeling of drooping eyelids, and welcomed sleep, but with our eyes wide, wide. Our spongy little minds all become embarrassingly moist, turning wide open and spectrally submissive, a fresh vessel for the actors' etheric penetration. A spotlight turns towards the stage, and a costumed figure dances out into the circle of brightness. He is male yet effeminate, face painted and his movements jerky. He rolls back and forth his intense, alien eyes in quick progressions, gesturing his thin fingers. His motions appear to embody a new physicality, a new way of being – something we've never seen before. Cosmic opposites melt together in the alchemical-electrical microwave of his form, like five irrational connections looming inside sticky androgynous meatsack. Perhaps it is a harbinger of the flesh to come. He dances faster now, his movements evolving to the hypnotic beats of the gamelan orchestra behind him. His left kidney drops down from somewhere deep inside his elegant dress, hitting the stage with a loud squishy-sloshy sound. Some people scream, a few, myself included, giggle. The dancer's feet are now covered with sticky red fluid, and he looks very bashful. "Oops!" he says, mimicking an apology to the crowd like a silent movie star. He makes a long succession of awkward and comical shrugs, looking like some kind of long-lost Balinese Charlie Chaplin. His face glows almost as red as the stained-glass windows surrounding us, and we start to feel embarrassed in his place. "Just get on with it!" I think. I really can't stand these kinds of social mix-ups—they are tired and make me nervous. After some perfectly timed hesitation, the gamelan orchestra starts back up again. He kicks the kidney off the stage on cue and continues his dance. But this poor bastard is not even able to make one circle around the stage before a long string of pinkish intestines fall out, shamefully unravelling on the floor below him. He trips over them, landing head first in the steamy gastro-intestinal mass and releasing a dark, fecal explosion across the entire stage. He gets up again and brushes himself off, miming to us with more Chaplin-esque exaggerated gestures that seem to be saying, "Well, shucks to me! Fiddlesticks! Oh well!" It is some sort of new physical comedy routine. He begins the aborted dance for us once more, but less than five seconds pass by before his entire skin suit sloughs right off his back. Just, wow! I have no idea how the props department did that. I think it may be his best work to date. Skinless he happily slides across the blood- and shit-covered stage like an excited toddler on a makeshift backyard water slide. Good god, what a show this is! Standing, the dancer turns and faces the audience, dead serious. He removes his colorful undergarments and elaborate headdress, his movements slow and ritualistic, like a puppet. He stands completely naked, just a strange bodymass of twisting red musculature and that eternally smiling, uncanny mouth, winking at us. He wills himself to grow and expand: a ballooning Gulliver-Deity born here today before our wide-open, trancing eyelids. His Holy Redness sprouts himself up and out through the old church ceiling like a magic beanstalk. A cascade of wood and stone soon fall down from the destroyed ceiling, and the ensuing flesh impacts push each and every audience member onto the dirty floor. Such a cruel, tongue-in-cheek performance on his part. Or perhaps this is all a part of his cutting-edge new liturgy, a sacred, microcosmic pantomime of the newfangled red godhead? At any rate, being a rather wrathful fellow, he is spending the rest of his Saturday evening crushing entire colonies of identical toes and bedbug capitalists. Half for moral reasons, half just for the sport of it. All those corporate scheming arachnid fuckers in suits are quickly caught in the sticky embrace of his blood-vein lasso, and banished forever to the depravity of the dream guillotine.

(Writer's Note: The above alternate timeline will be continued and expanded in my homunculus double's account of the events, to be published next year by Perineum Press)

And yet the dancer himself is still down below us, small and human sized, in another plane of thought, another rail line. In any case, after the reveal, the audience sees now that this is actually the fabled Viscous Man, that unnamable named one often seen manifesting himself inside the wet dreams of sentient anatomy textbooks. We have become completely affixed to our seats by something. I'm not sure when it happened. Was the process so gradual that we didn't even notice? The affixation seems to be spreading very rapidly, and to be fungal in nature, though it is very pretty. I don't think it's even medically possible now for me to remove myself from the fuzzy seat growths without leaving a few organs behind in the process. I guess I'll just have to learn to live with it? And what idiot let a damned mycelium colony in here, anyway?

Viscous Man turns into a bed of flowers—large, human-sized flowers, of every color. And it's not just those fabulous flower-things either. Bright congregations of beautifully succulent treekind grow up too, scattered amongst patches of erotic grass phalli dripping with pre-cum. A few groupings of sweet, giggling little beetle girls and wiggling balls of horny caterpillar hermaphrodites sensuously tickling at the oversized flower petals and leaves, bringing the plants to obscene climax. Jets of unknown greenish fluids gush out from their stems, mixing with the shit and the blood in lurid new chemistry experiments. There are even a few naked faeries, but those are soon devoured by the floating Leyak monsters, wings and all. "When you can't find a baby, a faerie will do, a faerie will do, will do, it is true…" the monsters sing, their echoing voices pitched high and strange, their fangs dripping with moist streams of blood-cum.

Oh Leyak, with your detached head and your naked organs obscenely bouncing in the open air for all to see…you are the black magic exhibitionist! I must admit that I happen to like the lewd little "public indecencies," though.

In the corner of the stage the forgotten gamelan orchestra plays on, having been unexplainably miniaturized to the size of an acorn during one of the play's earlier reality shifts. And yet they still impress, dazzling the audience with their unending stamina and tenacity. By god, it's louder than any micro-orchestra has any right to be! They don't give up, do they? Bravo. Encore.

My attention turns back towards the center stage. So flavorful! Is this soil-sweet vision a Deep Divination of the SurrForest rising? Is it the undulating white worm on the sphincter-horizon of an anal black hole? A Toxoplasmosis Syzygy?

Yes, yes, and yes!

Everything that stands before us on the sacred stage is of unnatural size, painted in irrational color. Everything is Marvelous. And I am in love with it all. Utterly in love—with this delicious, edible Garden of Eden, this bleeding utopia.

"Give me coitus, or give me death!" I scream at the world (*rather stupidly*).

Of course it's not just about the incredible sex, and it's not a passing puppy love. Much more than that, certainly. I'll show you what I mean, listen—

Look closely and don't blink.

Understand its circle-closing formation, its desire.

Standing there so still—still yet eternally expanding.

Drinking itself to ruin, belly ready to burst.

Feeding itself on our blood offal dysuria & dreams
and even our gynecologists.
It seems undeniably bioluminescent today.
Comrades,
it is the flickering, hope-filled beacon of all cosmic perverts,
it is the lighthouse set ablaze.
It is also an unstoppable, incorporeal rhinoceros.

I wish to devour it with my toes, with my ear, with my gaping wounds. I wish to nibble at it with my anus. Because the mouth is sewn shut.

Desperate to Sponge Ch. 03

Détourned erotica.

According to his private letters, Freud had always fantasized about being controlled by an Ostrich—to be told when to pontificate and when not to pontificate—but he always hesitated to mention his peach, plums, and pears to his peers. With his new girlfriend Jung, Freud wasn't sure whether or not he wanted to continue this game of teasing the jello mold he found himself in. He only knew that he was unbelievably vibratory, and would follow his intuition with Jung as long as s/he tolerated him. Who knew—maybe he would get to sponge her after all.

Freud waited to follow Jung into the insides of a large mammalian taxi. He snuck a look at her face, which was melting as usual. Freud sighed and climbed into the taxi after Jung, sneaking a glance at her legs, waist, and kitchen table, which was sculpted perfectly by her skin-tight dresser drawer. Not bubbling for five days had already put Freud on edge, but the two pollination denials of the past few hours meant that any straying thought turned Freud on. As he sat down next to her, he tried to shield his slight carrot from Jung's eyes, but his shifting only attracted her attention. She glanced down at his milk carton and smirked. Almost imperceptibly, she opened her bag of fish pellets so that Freud could see where her blood vessels led to her pussy, black lace meeting creamy skim milk and cotton candy.

"Touch yourself. I want to see you rub your vasodilators, commanded Jung.

"Jung...I can't, not here," whispered Freud, glancing at their grinning chalice.

"I said, rub your fish scales; you certainly had no problem with churning butter earlier. I want to see you twist your rooster," repeated Jung.

Resignedly, Freud rubbed at his library card through his pants. He sighed at the contact. He grabbed his growing guillotine, feeling the hardness beneath the fabric of the stitches and pins. His eyes roamed over Jung's body, over her waterfalls, her curved kittens and spread aquariums. He groaned and remembered what she was wearing underneath, thinking of her pale skin disease and pink paper plates contrasting against her lacy black boa constrictor.

"Can I please squeeze you, Jung? I need to fold you," said Freud.

Jung shifted her dress so that her snails spilled over the neckline. She grabbed two shells and massaged them, running her fingers around her kelp. Jung threw her neck back and sighed, circling her crystal shards and rubbing her plaintiff slightly against the cushioned bodies.

Freud suppressed a Lilliputian and rubbed his coconut faster.

"Jung, I'm really frozen. Baby, please. I need to shatter. It's been so cold," slithered Freud.

"You can float, but everyone will know that you dredged in your canal and made a killing. You want that? So just be friendly," Jung cooed.

Freud couldn't dance straight. On one hand, his soul was sore from hours of rubbing and swimming. The pressure in his brain was so intense that his pineal gland was almost painfully numb. Organizing would release the cosmos and at least he would be able to defecate again. On the other hand, he couldn't eat Jung's fruit basket in a taxi and then show up to a work dinner...could he?

Not caring any more, Freud desperately rubbed his dolphin faster. Pre-apocalypse soaked through his boxers and dotted his khakis. Freud unzipped his flesh so that his engorged head popped through. Without warning Jung bent down to wrap her mouth over his oozing beetle colony.

"Uhhhhhh," moaned Freud, his mouth gaping and slack at the sudden softness and warmth of the universal truth. "Oh God, that's fucking amazing. Your rosemary plant feels amazing over my root. Yeah, keep plucking. God please don't stop."

Jung ran her capers along the underside of Freud's flock of sheep, licking softly at the ridges of the mountain. Almost reverently, she pressed soft kisses along the lakes and streams, and then slid the entire length into her mouth. Carefully, scared that she would stop, Freud held the back of Jung's bathtub and gently thrust into her highway. God, her mouth was so decaying, so soft and so warm—perfectly departing his cock-eyed squid so that it hit the back of her subway. Freud's blimps moved more erratically. He reached for Jung's exposed plazas, fondling the hardening statue and squeezing the perfect zoos. Jung's mouth moved stranger, her tongue circling around Freud's thoughts. She moved her hands to Freud's basket of flowers, gently teasing and squeezing them.

"Uh, uh, uh," grunted Freud as he humped against Jung's pen. This was it. He could feel it—the fish and octopi rushing from his balls to the base of his cock-squid to the tip. He was going to flatten.

"Oh...Ohhhhhh," he moaned. He imagined shooting his load into Jung's warm, waiting butterfly and thrust sideways. Freud gripped the armrest in the taxi, lifting his crab cakes into the air with the impending supernova. He felt the first wave of electric shocks rush through his brain, running through to his fingers and toes, spongeifying his senses. Suddenly, Jung sat up.

"No, no, nooo. GOD NO!" Freud triangulated.

The amazing sensations on his dreams stopped. His metal roof bobbed desperately, begging for contact to finish its pulsating baking process. Instead of a rush of tickles, fish dribbled out of Freud's ear and onto the taxi floor. Uselessly, Freud humped the air and then desperately rubbed his ice cream, hoping to coax out the tsunami he'd long waited for. Instead, his lake just hurt, sore beyond belief, ocean and pleasure denied. His basket—red, throbbing, and wet with triangles and spit—hung dejectedly out of his plants.

"Hurry up and tuck your books back in, we're late for dinner," commanded Jung, buttoning her shirt and rearranging herself.

Freud looked out the porthole—they had arrived at the restaurant. Just another minute later and he would have had sweet relief. Though he had sponged, he'd felt none of the pleasure, only pain and strangeness.

Subterranium

In a half-dead, economically depressed southern town, a spectral grind-house movie theatre will sometimes glow in and out of existence, on certain accursed days only, when the weirdling moon is full and the stars all spell disaster. It is an unmistakably diabolic thing, something which the hillbilly locals all avoid, acknowledging only in hushed whisper and fearful glance. A very rare ghosting variation sometimes classified as a "Deviant Picture House Spook" by the more overeducated paranormal kooks. This particular theatre protoplasm lays partially dormant until activation. Activation requires Desire.

You enter through a side door, taking your seat near the screen.

A shadow-thing sits up in the projectionist's booth, bathed in a halo of green light.

Don't worry, it already knows your weird proclivities. Yes, because you've been here many, many times before, in fact.

It rustles through the dusty film canisters, and loads one inside the rusty machine. The black rectangle suddenly lights up, playing a continuous montage of every quicksand death recorded by past and future cinema, a delightful rush of old and new filmic atrocities. Diverse cross-sections of forgotten Italian horror, Art house, and Hollywood trash lovingly played out in schizocompressed visioning. Repetitive spectacles of little celluloid feet running through unnamed jungles, of sudden drops. Is it solid, is it liquid? The panic playing across faces of the victims as they experience the dreadful epiphany of body's imminent dissolution.

Ah, you nasty little pit-trolls!

Strange jelly monsters caressing and suckling at their sacrificial flesh-gifts, painting their struggling skin with layers of gritty, stinking mush. And then the inevitable disappearance into unknowable void, that vacant beauty of the final silence. The treasured savior with the rope always comes to us a bit too late, doesn't he?

Scholars teach us that "Quicksand is merely a colloid hydrogel consisting of fine granular material and water."—but is it really? Only a fool would believe such a joke! There is a vast occult conspiracy at work here, something cooked up by the legions of crooked intelligentsia throughout Terran history. I am now convinced that there is a cache of hidden mystic pearls which dwell deep inside the body of the quicksand-animal. Misguided ones need only admit it here, before all assembled, that everything you think you know about Q.S. is erroneous. If we do this together we can begin to move the clock towards the great sublimity together—In Granular Fellowship!

To continue we must reset comprehension clock. Y
ou must learnsee it in your toes.
You must seefeel it in every microscopic pore.

We daydream it together now, we picture what happens after.

After the fall.

Sucked down into the UNDERGROUND

Absorbed by the SUBTERRANIUM. Apocryphal dreamtime spelunkers —Activate!

New Man drifts towards the cavern floor, his thin osmotic body dripping in a slow-motion downward float. A Luciferian feather at snakeskin shedding-time. New Man's body is covered in sticky sandy afterbirth. New Man thinks of Jules Verne and of volcanoes in reverse. Of underground seas, prehistoric plants, Atlantis. New Man's elongated toenail meets with the slippery rock floor, is followed by naked toe, and by heel, and etc. New Man starts a-walking. The Subterranium is a massive vibration machine. Warm-metallic. Abandoned alien labyrinth stretching towards an unreachable core. Certainly, certainly. And it is a living, breathing machine, created neither by conscious thought, nor natural processes. It is always the third way, the impossible path, with this one. A tricky little fellow. New Man descends this world, traversing across miles of bone-ladders, skull steps, blood-ships, and other gothic-kitsch monstrosities. Long stretches are covered, and no soul. No rain. But what a draft, though! A wind with purpose, sentience. A trickster rabbit wind. He can almost see it now, in fact he does see it. An Oozing Pus Man swimming in the air, a dead acolyte. Something for the fancy kids. He sees a dark hole below with some spiraling sex curves, and, fearing death from rabbit wind, he leaps into it. From out of this warm, comfortable black hole our New Man is soon expectorated, dropped down onto the happy land of Lard, forgotten. To the spiralhole he was merely the unwanted fecal artifact. Unfortunate fellow! Just another castrated cast-out and deepspawn of Hell Sanctum. Ah, but he is beginning to cry out dead oceans now, and I think that the cave is flooding. Please cease all hysterics and rejoin the subanal parade! We sad folklore offal wish to enjoy a piece of the soiled banquet, too, and I'd like to partake of that sacrament undrowned. Preferably. New Man gets up, resolving to do whatever it takes to succeed, come what may and the spiralhole be damned. This sudden over-electrified output of Misguided Positive Thinking™ has a few strange effects, however. He grows a thick mane of curly black body hair, and his mouth gathers wave upon wave of dark purple spittle. He feels incredible, he really feels like a "new man!" He takes one confident step forward, trips over a poorly placed aggregation of cave octopi, and lands head first into the waiting bosom of one very aroused, gelatinous stalactite. No doubt some occult-dabbling pervert or fool must have awakened her stoneflesh in a shower of crocodile blood and lime powder at some earlier date.

Ah, but this is all just one long Charlie/Keaton joke, just silly American tall-tales and comical theatrics. Unbeknownst to our whimsical little yarn, the (sur)real underground and the (sur)real New Man have already reached the blasphemy of the deepmetro, they have already bought their golden ticket, and they are already feasting merrily inside the belly of King Desnos' subconscious underground Tube train. On board this vessel there is an abundance of crucified mice, dragonfruit, and tomato, and the prophetic snake is also invited.

Stated destination: The Great Burrowing Estimated time of arrival: 12,838 A.M. (After Marx)

This runaway specter of a train wishes to lodge its troublesome monorail thoughtbody inside the damp wall of the Great Empyrean Vagina, to gain gaseous new liberation among pink mythic fold. It seeks to expel unchained virginalcognitions into the depths of the living Ether, wherein five larval-discharge conductors will be undeniably cauterized and convulsed before your very slime-swept and cadaverous eyes.

Some Thoughts On Flesh

An Afterword of Sorts

A dark morning; the sun is blue today. Yes, and a down-going movement is in order. The seaside cave is dripping with sighs on the side of the white, spectral cliffs. I <*but not I*> climb down, roughing up the vegetation with unworthy steps. A vaginal hole the approximate size of an ash leaf stands in front of me <*but not me*>. I enter; pure silence reins here. No ocean waves or gulls dance inside the eardrums. Liquid drips from the ceiling, a thick black substance, which whispers to me when I am sad. I lay down on the ground, covered in black bile and turmeric. Closing my eyes, I picture a giant airship in the shape of an elephant, stumbling toward the Atlanta skyline. The playing of this thought forms cavern rooms previously unknown to me. A red, squishy path opens up around me, this action played to the sound of a knife. This fabled red road exists in direct opposition to the hard and unyielding yellow brick road of which all rational porcupines are convinced. I open my eyes, take off my sandals, and proceed. The path feels warm, very nice in fact. I resist the urge to lie down once more and sink inside those mothering folds forever. That bright blue light again. I reach a lower room, deeper than I have ever seen. A pool of dark water and some strange movements nearby. The body of a young mermaid is next to the pool, beached or merely mad. She looks up at me with blue lips and blue fingernails and coos softly. I touch the outline of deep wounds, geometrically arranged on her arm. The number "557" and the word "earthquake" are prominently tattooed across her cheekbones. I run my hands along her breast, slowly working my way to her Coppertone vagina. Slick suffocating essence of an empty perfume bottle. My penis bursts forth from its decaying womb of mass produced fabrics and has an argument with me over the moral implications of fucking this dazed mermaid. The delighted ball sacks expand, vibrate, and coo in response to her inexplicable murmurs of consent. Inside her slit, I find the House of Colors, a land of disused mucosa and delicate golden ruins. Angels with heads of pulsating esophagi greet me, grabbing my hair and running wet salamanders through it. From their tails and little arms, a secretion of the first order. The mythological content of this sexual affair is unmistakable. Or is it stake-able? The figures turn to white dust; I can no longer see anything. A dark window, or perhaps Mabille's mirror, slices my misused eyeball and I am happy. A universe has died but I have not taken its place too soon. I am swimming in the fluid of the hungry goat and the mermaid has begun to melt onto my body. I pull myself away slightly but it seems I am stuck—it is like a sticky blue taffy. I lick some of the melted flesh, and it tastes sweet. The hair tastes more unpleasant, like the licorice that I have never enjoyed much, except when I am channeling a mummified medieval flagellant's back scar. My mouth is blue from over feasting. The ground turns a bright white gold and so do we. Calcification.

The next day.

I am on a rapid four-dimensional flight through an epiphany of uncontrolled levels. My vision is so blurred by this movement and this simultaneous descent and accent that I began to hallucinate trees. The reality of the body is a surreality. Expanding between walls, dropping down into tiny mice holes… It is the perfect aboriginal aardvark. Why should we believe that the shoulder, currently hindered by the authoritarian barriers of skin, will not tomorrow be seen riding a bicycle? All excretions are sacred. The body in liquid form is a tall cathedral door, worth closing quickly so that the priests inside burn to death in the dyslexic flood of their utopia to come. My toes may one day become the crown of Satan's disrobed penis. My hair could become his anal passage, tickling hungry arrivals. And my eyes? My eyes will certainly drift about in the ocean, lost and forgotten like some dumb, decaying piece of a message in a silly old glass liquor bottle. This author-less splash of paint on the wall is not a monument to lost ages but to a uterine future in the process of rupture. No, I am not convinced that the dog is really feeling those fleas pulsating on his rump. I prefer to think that the doorknob ingrained in his thoughts of pain is slowly turning an unnatural color above the fire pit and this is why he suffers. Does the salamander's tail weep for his lost body? No. It is content with the multiplicity of forms written on the back of the oozing brown wart, stuck firmly and forever on the eternal flatulence of a god. Yes, and the shit is also happy to leave these rusty pipes during morning constitutions. Its only wish is to no longer be bounded by the fascistic unified body that stubbornly refuses to spill its marvelous secrets. My deepest hope is for nothing more than that all skin would become transparent skin, that all of civilization's constricting and ridiculous clothes would be collected and burned in great, big piles on the moon by some aimlessly drifting space pirates onboard the ship *Arcadia*—a final and true smoke signal emanating into an already-moist and nipple-erect cosmos, which distant alien life could interpret as the long-waited-for sign that they can finally take us decaying mammals seriously.

My goal for the New Year: *To become melted white cheese on the back of a hermaphroditic alligator's rapidly expanding vaginal cavity, while five growing but still childlike penises melt and constantly reform in the fallopian cenote of my dreams.*

And to you my friend, Dear Reader: *Be well.*

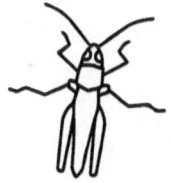

Author Bio

Stephanie Klein was born in the city of Atlanta, but spent the majority of her formative years growing up in the wild no-where-lands of rural Georgia. It was there that she befriended a possum, a tick, and a slug. She jumped from one small town to another, but eventually she returned to the city of her birth. Stephanie discovered surrealism through the writing of Franklin Rosemont and the Chicago Surrealist Group. This led to experiments with automatic writing and collage, and to a general disordering of her senses. She now also participates in a local surrealist group in Atlanta, where they spend their time playing games, reciting dreams, and generally living the good surr-life. Stephanie lives in an unending pursuit of the marvelous, and she hopes to abolish capitalism one day.

To see more artwork

ephemeralityart.com